POINTED LOVE

NIGHTWOOD CLAN SERIES BOOK 3

HARPER DAKOTA

Warning:
This book contains mature themes and is intended to be read by ages 18+. There is mention of rape, that resulted in a child, to a primary character. Please skip the Prologue if that is a trigger for you. Main character also suffers from anxiety, although this book does not delve deep into it. Contains sex, some curse words, paranormal and magical themes including fated mates. There are secondary characters that are a male/male couple.

Trademark Acknowledgements:
The author acknowledges all trademarks mentioned in the book, including:
Let's Get It On by Marvin Gaye
Bugs Bunny/Warner Bros.
Ticket To Ride

Cover Design by: Jay Aheer
Editing by: Lori Parks

To my family. I love you all.

POINTED LOVE

Emma is a vampire. She didn't start that way; she had been born human. Growing up in 1800s England, she worked on her parents' farm until she was attacked one day by a traveler. That day forever changed her family's lives and sent her life on a completely new course. Left with an amazing son, but a healthy dose of anxiety, Emma learns to navigate her new life.

Many years later, her son is an adult and is returning home after being away for a couple of years. Finding her close to death, Rolf transforms Emma into a vampire to save her life. Although being a paranormal doesn't cure her anxiety, it does gift her with visions of the future.

When her only child is put in danger from the very man who attacked her all those years ago, she travels across the ocean to help defeat the monster. Arriving in America, she moves into her son's home. There is safety in numbers, making it smart for them to stay together. Rolf opens his house to his friends, as it is large enough that everyone has their own room. They all find something while living together...a family. A visitor to the house reveals that Fate has decided to gift her a mate of her own, but will her past allow her to claim him?

Doc has secrets that he has been keeping for hundreds of years. To embrace his new mate and form trust between them, he must find a way to share those secrets with her. After being alone for so long, Doc is ready to do anything to win his mate's affections.

Pointed Love is the third book in the Nightwood Clan series. There is some overlap between books. Although it can be read as a stand-alone, you will get the most out of the book after reading the first two books in the series, as many of the characters make an appearance.

NOTE: *Pointed Love* references the main female character being raped, resulting in a child. There are two scenes: one does not get into the details of the event, the other depicts her struggling, but the act is not finished on page. Please skip the Prologue if this might upset you.

PROLOGUE

Emma stood in the doorway for a moment, enjoying the last little bit of shade and looked out over her family's farm. Her mother was already in the vegetable garden looking for items that were ready to pick. As Emmaline headed toward the chicken coop to gather the eggs, she saw the smoke coming from her father's workshop. He worked as the town's blacksmith and farrier. She was curious what he was working on, but she was no longer allowed to enter the forge. Hopefully it would be a little cooler today so her father could get a lot of work done. She knew he was worried about completing a few jobs.

Her older brother had been her father's apprentice, although she had been allowed to play in the workshop and help occasionally. One day her brother cut himself on an old piece of metal and an infection took hold. The local doctor had been no help in treating him and his wound kept getting worse until finally his body had no more to give. It took many painful months before her brother passed; months of watching him not being able to open his jaw wide enough to eat anything that required chewing, seeing him suffer through painful muscle spasms, and sometimes helping clean up when he would lose the ability to control his bowels. His eyes would fill with tears when he could not control his own body, an apology in his eyes. She had made sure to spend any extra time she had with him, especially on those days. Eventually the disease took control of his lungs and he struggled to breathe. After her brother passed away, she wasn't allowed near the tools. Her father told her, "It had taken one child, I will not let it take another."

Shaking the memories off, she started gathering the eggs again and placed them inside on the table. Grabbing the milking bucket, she went over to say good morning to her favorite cow. They also had a bull, but so far there had been no sign of a calf coming this season. They had a calf last year and had sold it to another farmer. Emmaline was looking forward to another. They had the softest noses. She was hoping her parents would keep the next baby that came along; the baby animals were one of her favorite things on the farm.

"Hello, pretty girl," Emmaline said softly as the cow came over to the fence. She slipped the cow the carrot end that she had saved from dinner the night before. The bull came over to get a treat as well, and she fed him another small piece. He was a large animal, but he had always been gentle with her. They had grown up together on the farm, he was used to her.

Emmaline milked the cow while distracting her with some additional vegetable trimmings. She wanted to make butter today. She may have enough to sell some in town, which would help.

"Emmaline! Can you get a bucket of water, please? The garden is getting very dry," her mother called out.

"Yes, Mother," she replied before putting the milk in the house and getting another bucket.

As she walked to the well, she could hear her father working in his shop, the sounds of metal clanging a familiar tune. She let herself daydream a bit as she pulled the rope for the bucket up. Henry, a boy from a neighboring farm, had been nodding at her lately when he saw her in town. He was handsome enough, she supposed. Although she was at the age to marry, she was not ready to leave her family. Her mother had been devastated when her brother died, and her father would not have anyone to help him. He was being stubborn and did not want to take another apprentice. Maybe if Henry decided to court her, then he could move to her family's farm if they married. She snorted. Not likely. She would just have to wait for the right man, Emmaline decided. Pouring the water into her bucket, she noticed that the air had gone quiet and still. The hairs on her arms stood up and she had an uneasy feeling.

"Mother? Father?" she called out, looking around. Grabbing the bucket, she prepared to run home. She would ask Father to come back to the well with her. There may be a predator in the area; the air was never this quiet.

A man suddenly appeared before her, causing her to drop the water bucket. She lunged for it, but it fell down into the well with a splash. She eased around the other side of the well, hoping to put some distance between her and this stranger. She had not seen him before; he was dressed smartly like the other large landowners and the elite in the area. His dark brown hair was neatly styled, but his eyes... Those eyes gave her chills. The hazel should have been attractive, but they were void of emotion. This man *was* the predator and her instincts screamed at her to run.

"My father is at his workshop. I will let him know you are here," she said as she began to walk backward toward home.

"I have no need for him," the man stated. His voice was deep and struck a chord of terror through her.

She nodded before grabbing her skirts and running toward home as fast as she could. She only got a few feet before she felt a hand grab her arm and yank her back.

"Not so fast. You, I have a need for." He towered over her, his head blocking the sun.

"Sir! Let me go. I need to get home." She tried pulling out of his grasp, but he held her tight.

"No," he replied simply.

"Father!" Emmaline screamed. She did not want this man touching her. She slapped him with her free hand, kicking out, trying to get away.

The stranger laughed before backhanding her. She felt the pain blossom across her face and tasted blood from her lips. Spitting at him, she aimed her next kick between his legs. He moved so fast it seemed like he was a blur.

"Uh uh," he scolded her. He seemed to be enjoying this.

"Father!" she screamed again. He must hear her, she needed him.

The man punched her stomach, causing her to double over.

"Quiet now," he demanded. "Hmmm. I think you will make good breeding stock," he added, thoughtfully. "Your features are attractive enough and you have some life to you."

"My daughter is no one's breeding stock." Emma heard her father's voice behind her. "Leave. Now."

"I do not think so," the stranger replied, his voice cold and hard.

The man had released her as her father spoke and Emmaline slowly inched her way toward her father, trying not to make any sudden moves and attract the stranger's attention again. Her father was holding a hammer and a long pair of tongs. She knew how heavy those were. A faint thread of hope entered her heart as soon as her father arrived. He was the strongest man she knew, the years of working with metal had made his muscles quite solid. This stranger would leave them alone now, there was no way he was stronger than her father.

Her father raised his weapons, gesturing with his head for

her to run back home. As she turned to run, she heard her father gasp in pain and turned back around. The stranger had grabbed his arm, stopping his swing. As her father brought his other hand up, the man tightened his fist causing her father to scream in pain. She could hear the bones breaking from where she stood. Simply from squeezing his hand. Her father dropped to his knees, but still tried to swing at the monster. The man grabbed the tongs as they fell and hit her father on the side of his head. Her father did not make another sound as he collapsed to the ground, blood seeping from his head.

"Now where were we?" the stranger asked, as if he had not just easily overpowered and gravely injured her father. "Oh yes, my broodmare. I will achieve immortality and the name Vlad will be remembered. You are going to give me offspring to help me, I know it. All my other attempts have been duds, failures. We will see if you can do any better."

A blur of motion and she felt herself falling to the ground, a hand at her throat, squeezing and holding her in place while his other hand untied his pants and rucked her skirts up.

"We are going to head south, purchase a new farm. Henry's father is going to buy our land. We will change our last name. You are going to pose as a widow, so that there is no shame thrown at you for having a child out of wedlock. We are going with you; I can still help on a farm, even if I cannot smith anymore. This creature will not ruin your life, Emmaline," her father told her, sitting at their table.

It had been a couple of months since that monster came to their property. Her father had recovered but his hand could no longer close in a grip, and his sight was blurry on the side where he was hit. He couldn't work as a blacksmith any longer. Emmaline was terrified to go past the safety of the house. They had simply told the village that her father had been attacked by a traveler. While they had been supportive during his recovery, she knew the same consideration would not be given to her if they knew the truth. Her mother had helped her as she healed from the attack. She had woken up in the fields, her mother sobbing over her and her father. There was a bag of coins dropped by her body. She had bled for a bit and had bruises on her arms and neck. She even had teeth marks on her thighs. Those had been so deep that they scarred.

When a month or so had passed and her menses hadn't arrived and she started feeling ill, she went to her mother in tears. Their small village would not care about the circumstances, they would only care that she would be with child out of wedlock. While moving to a whole new area worried her, she could see her father's plan was a good one. Posing as a widow, she would have more freedom to raise her child without the pressure of marrying. Marriage no longer held any appeal; she did not want anyone to touch her again. Maybe the monster wouldn't be able to find her if they moved. Emmaline didn't want him anywhere near her child. They had never used the coins the man had left, not wanting anything from him. When she tried to give them to her father to help with the expenses of their new home, he told her to keep them for when he and her mother were gone from this world, to use them to keep her freedom.

Her precious child was born at their new home with only her mother's aid. Emmaline did not want even the village's doctor to assist. When she saw her son for the first time, she fell in love. He had none of the evilness of the man who attacked her. Rolfston was a good child, always helping her on the farm. When her parents passed away, it was just the two of them for a while. He didn't show any interest in moving away to spread his wings and she was grateful to keep him close. She never told him the real story behind his father; she never wanted him to know how he was conceived or to feel guilt over something neither one of them could control.

Vlad eventually found them. Through the years, she thought she caught glimpses of Vlad. He would always smirk at her before disappearing. Occasionally he would sneak behind her, whisper in her ear and then trip or shove her. He never approached when Rolfston was nearby, so Emma had no idea what he was after. When her son turned twenty-five, the monster returned and took her son with him. He threw another bag of coins at her, telling her he had known she would be "good breeding stock." She demanded to see her son, but he told her he was "resting." During the years he was gone, her precious boy would send back money or trinkets for her with letters of his travels. Rolf kept saying he would return when it was safe, but she had no idea when that would be or what the danger was.

She had been lucky enough that they had hired a farmhand a couple of months before Rolfston left. The man continued to stay with her on the farm. She had enough money to pay him a small wage and they worked well enough together. She had been wary of having him on the farm by herself, but over time she learned that Jacob was a good soul. He was gentle and kind to her. He was a smaller man, only a few inches taller than her, but he made her feel safe the more she got to know him. They became friends of a sort during the first few months that Rolfston was gone. After about a year of him working on the farm, she heard a commotion out in the yard and went to see what was disturbing the chickens. It wasn't a fox like she had thought, but instead it was Jacob and another man near the chicken coop, kissing. The other man was a traveler who was just passing through and had run off once they spotted her. Jacob had been a combination of mortified and terrified that she would tell someone or fire him. It was no one's business who he spent time with, she had reassured him. After inviting him inside the main house, she poured them each a drink and told him her own secret, the truth behind her son's birth. The world was a place that was not inviting or safe for those it deemed inferior, so they banded together. They told the village that they were betrothed, keeping anyone from questioning their friendship or their private lives. It had been so nice having a friend, someone she could talk to. She was wary of other men due to her history, but she felt safe enough to go into town when Jacob was with her. He became her best friend and she thought of him as part of her family.

Three years after taking her son away, the monster returned. He appeared suddenly, no footsteps announcing his arrival. Close to twenty-eight years had passed since she had first seen him, when he had destroyed her father's livelihood and impregnated her. Emma thought that she had aged well, but this man hadn't changed at all. She had no idea how it was possible, but he didn't have one single wrinkle to show the passage of time. Everything about him was the same, except his eyes were even colder, if that was possible. He sneered at her, telling her how weak her son was, that he refused to rise to greatness like his father. She stood her ground, responding that she was glad her son was nothing like him. That she was proud of her boy for not tormenting people.

"Did you know, he is almost home?" he asked casually. "I think that after abandoning me, I should leave him a welcome home present."

Emmaline had started carrying a knife with her after the attack years ago and she grabbed it. She would not make it as easy as last time. Jacob was off in town, trading butter for some oats and other things they had needed. She was glad he was not here.

"I am a little old to be your broodmare again," she told him.

"Eh. It's more the fight I enjoy, taking what I want. It gets my blood flowing, it is a euphoria like nothing else," Vlad said, eyeing her body speculatively. "You did provide me one offspring, maybe you could do another. I hate starting over and have not had much luck creating viable options with anyone else."

"No."

He laughed at her then and lunged toward her. She swiped at him with her knife, hoping to slow him down. How was he moving this fast? He blurred when he moved. Emma heard him hiss and knew that she had at least cut him a little bit.

"You little bitch. Now you are going to pay for that. I will not go easy on you like last time," he threatened.

She ran out further into the yard, putting more space between them. If she could get to the barn, she would at least have a wall and a door as a barrier. The house was too far away. She glanced over her shoulder, trying to find him. Emmaline had almost reached the door when he appeared in front of it.

"I do not think so," Vlad said, shaking his head at her.

Suddenly a hand was around her neck, squeezing until she was gasping for air. His other hand threatened to break her wrist, he was squeezing so hard. She lost feeling in her fingers and heard the clink as the knife dropped and hit the ground. He let go of her throat to fumble with the front of her skirt. She frantically twisted her body, kicking and trying to get loose. His grip was like iron, there was no breaking his hold. Her kicks were ineffective, although she could feel her feet making contact.

"Release me!" she demanded, panicking internally.

He just grunted as he reached toward the ties of his pants. She moved, trying to bite him, and spat in his face. He let go of his pants to cuff the side of her head, causing her ears to ring. She almost blacked out. Before she could recover from the hit, he pulled her hands behind her back and shoved her face-first into the wall. As Vlad reached down to drop his pants, he kept one hand on her arms, pulling them tight behind her, pressing her against the barn. Straining and moving any way she could, Emma managed to get one arm free.

"Emmaline!" she heard Jacob call out and she saw him running toward them from the house.

She yelled at her friend. "Run! He will kill you!" She reached behind her and jabbed at Vlad's eyeball, trying to injure him.

"I certainly will, my little pet. You are my broodmare and no one else's, although I do not smell him on you," Vlad said, sniffing her. He ripped her petticoats and started to force himself into her. She never wanted this, she thought angrily as she kept struggling, desperate to keep him from getting further into her body.

As he pulled back to thrust his hips, she moved, dislodging the tip from her entrance. There was a quick breeze followed by a sharp sound. Vlad grunted and stepped back from her.

"Run!" Jacob shouted as he lined up another shot. Vlad was bleeding, but he wasn't slowing down. Emmaline ran toward Jacob and tried to grab her friend so they could run together.

"Go, be safe. I will try to stop him," Jacob told her urgently, giving her a kiss on her forehead. He knew he may not survive this but wanted to give his dear friend a chance at escaping.

"But—" Emmaline started to protest.

"Go!" Jacob said again, pressing a different knife into her hands and giving her a push. He watched as she ran into the fields.

"I don't know who you are, but you need to leave my friend alone." He tried to stand his ground sternly.

He got off one more shot before he saw a blur of motion and then his throat was on fire. His last thought was of his friend, hoping she got away and would live.

Emma sobbed as she ran into the fields. She had an old shelter further back on the property. If she could get there, maybe she could hide from Vlad. There was another shot and then silence. She knew in her soul that her friend was gone. She was almost there when something tackled her from behind. Her head smacked into the ground, but she managed to hold on to the knife. Flipping onto her back she held the knife ready. Those cold dead eyes laughed down at her before he moved lightning-fast, her wrist now lying useless on the ground. She knew it was broken even though at the moment she couldn't feel it. Emma drew in a breath, mentally bracing herself and tried to get to her feet. If she was standing, she would have at least a little better odds. She didn't think she would live past this day, but she wouldn't give up without a fight. Getting to her knees, she felt a boot connect with her ribs, causing fire to spread across her chest. She coughed, blood coming out of her mouth. Gasping for breath, she couldn't draw in enough air.

"All you had to do was shut up and take it. Instead, your stupid beau and you caused me to lose my temper. Look what you made me do; now I cannot even use you for more offspring. Useless bitch. I am hungry and need to heal, so I suppose I have one final use for you. You can be my dinner and I will leave your body for your equally useless offspring to find. He should be here soon," Vlad said as he squatted next to her.

She felt his hands grab her hair and yank her head up to him. His teeth weren't normal, his canines large and sharp-looking. She screamed as he tore into her body. He bit her wrists, her arms, and where her neck met her shoulder. She could feel her body weakening even more, turning cold.

"Hmm, you may not make it until he gets here. Let's

extend your life a little longer, just long enough for him to see what happens when someone does not listen to me." The monster bit his own wrist, forcing her mouth open to take some of his vile blood into her. Her heart gave a valiant effort, speeding up from the lethargic pace it had been reduced to, but she knew death was coming. As the monster sped away, she thought she heard her precious son's voice one more time.

1

Emma woke with a start. The echoes of his voice still reverberating in her ears. The asshole liked to taunt her to this day. She was sure some people would say it was all in her imagination, but the coins she would occasionally find near her gate or tossed over the fence to land by her front door said otherwise. They were antique coins, not something someone would casually have in their pockets and would allow to fall out. The metal discs were a perfect match to the bag of coins he had left after the first attack. She had hired a witch to ward her property against evil, so Vlad could not come on the property again. The coins could be tossed over the line as they were an inanimate object. He was tenacious and when he wanted to torment her, he would wait until she left the grounds and would stalk her in town, shoving her from the shadows, whispering "broodmare" in her ear. The worst was when he would grab her from behind and break a bone; it was never something big enough to draw attention, a finger, her wrist, a toe. Her increased healing meant that her injuries were not noticed by the people in the village; bruises never lasted more than a couple of hours, bones were healed within a day or so. She never knew when he might show up again, it could be days or months. When it got to be too much, she would leave her home and move to a different location. She bought houses across Europe, hiding for a while and then selling them when she left. The reprieves were short, as he would eventually find her. She didn't like to be far from her main home and she always moved back. The ward meant that she felt a little safer here at least. She was of no use to him any longer since becoming a vampire, as paranormals had low birth rates, so she had no idea why he was still fixated on her. Emma suspected that the only reason Vlad had not killed her yet was because her death would guarantee that her son would never join his cause. From what she had heard, Vlad had not had much luck creating any other children; it was the only reason she could think of why he was still obsessed with Rolfston. She had been so relieved when her tormentor moved to America. There was now an entire ocean between them. Not that it would stop him for long if he really wanted to finish her.

She got up and made herself a cup of chamomile tea. Her heart was still beating fast. All these years later and she still had nightmares. After Jacob died, she kept more to herself. She stopped trying to maintain long-term friendships. If she didn't have close friends, Vlad could not come back to hurt them, she reasoned. Due to the years of Vlad's abuse, her anxiety and fear of men increased. Once he was in America, the harassment had gotten better. There was still the occasional coin or whispered word, but they were far less frequent. Some of them had been from Vlad when he was back in the country, some had been his minions when he was overseas, but in general it had greatly diminished. She slowly worked on her anxiety and leaving her home; it was a struggle, but she found herself being able to take short trips into town.

Then one day her precious son decided to move to America too. She couldn't bring herself to visit him; just knowing Vlad was in the same country was enough to keep her close to England. Rolfston and she still talked quite a bit and she loved that technology allowed her to video call him so she could see his face. For a while, she had been quite upset that he moved so far away. Rolfston eventually told her that he had been hoping that if he was in the same country as Vlad, the monster would keep his attention on him and leave Emma alone. She knew her son didn't know just how badly the harassment had been, but he must have witnessed one of the events.

Emmaline felt the edges of her vision turn gray and she put down her cup to grab the table. Her son had saved her life, turning her into a vampire, but the process had also given her a couple of gifts. The telepathy was useful, but the visions were the gift that generally popped up at inconvenient times. Oh! This vision made her smile though, a mate for her child. He deserved to find a good mate and this girl was so loving. She had a gift of her own, which would turn out to be useful, her instincts told her. The vision sped forward in time, showing her in America meeting her daughter-in-law in person.

She reached out to Rolfston through their mental link. It was handy being able to speak to her son without a phone, although the video calls were still her favorite. She couldn't wait to share some good news with him. She frowned as she found it blocked on his end. Emma politely tapped on the link, thinking maybe he was in the middle of something. When he didn't respond, she called his phone.

"Ah, my little broodmare. I am sorry our son cannot come to the phone now. I will let him know you called," the monster at the other end of the line said before disconnecting.

She frantically tried to call back, but it went straight to voicemail. Emma paced around the room, trying to think of a way to get in contact with her son. She opened her link all the way, focusing on where he lived. He continued to keep his side of the link locked down. With his phone now going directly to voicemail, she had no other way of reaching him. She had never asked for any contact information of his friends, something she now very much regretted.

Emma did the one thing she swore she would never do. She booked a plane ticket to America, intent on saving her son. The movies had totally lied when they always showed the hero grabbing a last-minute plane ticket and running to the rescue, she thought to herself, frustrated. She tried explaining to the airlines that it was a life-or-death situation, but without an official letter or confirmation from a hospital, they did not believe her. Two days! Two days was the earliest she would be able to get there.

Emma kept searching for a way to help him. Maybe if she could find someone who was open mentally, she could nudge them to Rolf's house or have them call the authorities. She sat, focusing on scanning the area around her son's house. There had to be someone... There! That was her son's mate nearby. She hoped the girl could hear her telepathically. Rolfston had let his guards slip today and she could sense how injured he was. He demanded she stay in England, which, of course, she did not agree to. She watched as the girl made her way to the house, the wards letting her through. The girl walked up the drive and paused by the front door.

'Go to the top floor, the left turret,' Emma told her, crossing her fingers that the girl could hear her clearly. She paused but went into the house.

'Get away. There is evil here. Run,' Rolfston urged, reaching out to the girl as well.

'Please, you must help him, or he will die! Save him for me,' Emmaline begged the girl.

"I will try," the girl whispered back, speaking aloud.

Emmaline watched as the girl walked up the flights of stairs to the turret. The monster was standing over her son, his poor body hanging from the ceiling, bruised, and broken.

'Evil,' she hissed, warning the girl not to get too close.

"Ah, another plaything for me," the monster in a man's form said as he began to move toward the girl with manic anticipation in his eyes. Rolfston growled and tried to grab at Vlad but could not move very far. Vlad merely laughed and said "another time" before vanishing out the window. Emma watched as the girl ran to her son and managed to get him down. Through their family link, she could feel the healing energy the girl was pushing into Rolfston's battered body. The healing took almost everything out of the girl and Emma watched concerned as she passed out next to her son.

'Rolfston…Rolfston!' She shouted at her son, trying to wake him up to help. This was his mate, he had to be able to save her too.

Rolfston slowly woke and gave the poor girl enough blood to help restore enough of her own energy that she would not die. He still needed to rest and drink to fully recover, but she did not want him to leave the girl alone. He should have some supplies in the house that he could use.

'You are going to stay put and watch over her. Do not even contemplate going out. The first thing you should do is reset the safeguards,' Emma warned her son.

'Yes, Mother,' he replied, sighing.

'I am not joking. You need to protect her. She is utterly defenseless.'

'I just did,' he muttered back.

'No, you helped her to heal her body. My son, I have been around on this earth longer than you have. Granted, you have been immortal a little longer, but I still have more experience than you have. Whether you see it yet or not, there is something there between you,' she insisted, trying to impress on him the girl's importance.

'What have you seen?' he asked, resignation in his tone.

'She is your destiny, your mate. You both need each other; neither can exist fully without the other,' Emma answered.

'*What else is there?*'

'*It is not for you to know yet. Time will reveal it to you. It could be disastrous if you found out too soon. Some things are meant to be in their own time.*' Emma hated not being able to tell him the whole truth, but some things really did need to work out on their own.

Rolfston sighed again. '*Mother? I would ask your help.*'

'*You need only ask,*' she reassured him. He was her only child, her beloved son. Of course, she would help.

'*My strength is not quite back all the way. Will you help me with the safeguards?*'

'*Go and feed. You will need your strength,*' she urged. She knew he always kept a few bags of blood on hand.

He hesitated before answering. '*I will later.*' Rolf looked reluctant to leave the room. Emma was happy that he was drawn to his mate already.

'*Rest then. I will make sure you both are safe,*' Emma promised.

'*Stay home, please. I am safe now. I would feel better if you were far away from him,*' Rolf demanded gently.

Emma paused, using their telepathic link to make sure he was telling the truth and was recovered enough to keep both of them safe. '*I will stay here for now, but only if you tell me if you are in danger again. I want to help.*'

'*Fine,*' he agreed grumpily.

She sensed when her son lay down and drifted to sleep next to the girl. Emma breathed a little easier, knowing he was safe. His friends would help as well, she knew. He only had to ask. They were all good boys.

What her vision showed her, what she didn't tell her son, was that eventually she would be moving to America and living with her son's family. She might not be needed now, but eventually she would be. She had so much to do! She had a long-term caretaker that lived in a small house on the property, so her house and the grounds would be taken care of.

She did not need a lot of her furniture and there were plenty of other things in the house that she would not bring with her. She resolved to start getting ready to move, even if it was months or years before that happened. It was amazing the amount of stuff one could amass over two hundred years. It was terrifying to leave the home that had always been there for her, but her son and daughter-in-law were worth moving for.

"Ma'am?" Emma heard a voice at the door. She was in the study, packing her favorite books to be shipped. She had thought that this would be the easiest place to start, but knowing she was going to be gone indefinitely seemed to make it harder for her to decide what to bring and what to leave here.

"Samantha…I have known you for what, fifty years now? Please call me Emma or Emmaline." Emma turned toward the door to see the caretaker/housekeeper standing in the doorway.

"I think it is closer to seventy-five years, ma'am…Ms. Emmaline."

Emma sighed to herself. Well, that was progress at least. Samantha was the closest thing she had to a friend. When they met, Emma had been in Scotland. She had been changing locations to avoid one of Vlad's minions. While she was exploring the new town, she had witnessed the poor brownie being harassed and had stepped in to rescue her. She still didn't know where she found the courage that day. When it was time to return home, Samantha decided to come with her. Emma had been so pleased when Samantha had found her own mate in a lovely gnome gentleman that lived in the local town. Emma had built them a house on her property, and it had been built to suit their shorter statures. Her friends had

had several children through the years, some of them staying around the farm and the local town, some of them traveling far away. It had been nice to have the sound of children running around the farm again.

Douglas had a background of working as a farrier, just like Emma's father. As farrier's grew out of style with the increased use of cars, Douglas had started using his black-smithing skills to create impressive statues and works of art, so Emma had also built him a workplace that had a studio room and a blacksmithing area. Due to the farming in the area, he still worked as a farrier as needed. Samantha helped Emma out around the farm and created wonderful quilts and woven blankets. She really would have been lost without the two of them. They were her only friends left in this world.

"I wanted to talk to you about the farm," Emma said, putting down a stack of books. "Rolfston's found his mate! She seems like such a lovely person, and I cannot wait to meet her."

"When are they coming to visit?" Samantha asked.

"No, I would be going to them," Emma started to explain.

Samantha gasped. "But what about—" she started to ask. Emma had warned her about Vlad and the ongoing problems before they left Scotland. She had wanted Samantha to have all the information to make the right decision for her.

"He is still there. He just attacked Rolf. His mate was the one that saved him. I had a vision though that shows me going there. I'm not sure when I will be leaving or when I would return. I may be gone for a long time. The deed is magical, so it will transfer automatically to my new name when it's time for my 'death.' All taxes and fees are set to be automatically paid. This is still your home if you want to stay. I am sure I will come back to visit at the very least, and hope-fully Rolf and Shaye will come too. I wanted to ask if you would still want to act as caretaker here?" Emma asked, holding her breath as she waited for an answer. She could tell that Samantha was talking to her mate through their bond.

"We will stay. It is our home and one of the older kids can come house-sit if we go on a trip ourselves. Don't you worry, Ms. Emmaline. We will keep your home safe and watch over the graves."

"Thank you both so much. I feel much better knowing it will be in good hands. I am going to start boxing some things to be shipped over to Rolfston's house. Is there anything you want me to leave? Do you want me to leave the animals or see if a neighbor will take them in?"

"We will take care of the beasts. The youngest likes feeding them every morning."

"I am glad she is still liking it. I will be only a phone call or email away. I'll make sure everything is set up to run smoothly before I go: human and animal food deliveries, annual vet visits, taxes and fees, your paychecks. If there is something you think I am missing, please tell me."

"I will go over our lists and make sure they line up," Samantha reassured her. "I am off to the market to get some things to make a stew for tomorrow's dinner. Was there anything you needed while I am out?"

"Not from the market, but I did want to talk to you about commissioning a blanket for Rolf and his mate."

"Give me an idea of what you want, and I will get started on it," Samantha replied with a smile as she walked out the door.

Emma went back to sorting her books. She thought maybe a pale gray and rich deep blue in a quilt would look nice for a mating gift. She was very relieved that Samantha and her family would stay on. They would still have the safety of their home and she would have the comfort of knowing this place would be here for her. There was a spell over the house that kept it protected and preserved, but she still felt better knowing that someone who loved it would also be watching over it.

Jacob would probably tell her it was time to move on, but this property had been the one constant in her long life. What had been a small farmhouse when Rolfston was growing up, had been added on to over the years and was now a lovely stone cottage. She still had a few farm animals and grew several of her own fruits and vegetables. This land was hers; it held her blood and tears, her parents and her dear friend from so long ago were buried here. She continued to look after them like they looked after her.

Emma was out in the garden, plucking some ripe tomatoes for a salad when another vision came over her. There was a field with decorations and a raised platform. Her son stood on the decking with his friends, facing several guests. Emma watched as herself, Shaye and another girl walked toward the ceremony area. That must be Tess, Emma thought to herself. Emma saw herself begin to speak, when Vlad suddenly arrived, armed and with his minions. However, Rolfston and his group were ready for them. She saw parts of the battle, but not all of it. As the vision ended abruptly, she had the sense they were winning. It looked like she needed to move up her timeline. She thought she would have more notice, but it looked like it was still just barely autumn in the vision.

"Samantha!" Emma called out. "It looks like I will be gone by mid-November." She needed to pack faster so that she would be ready in time.

2

Emma had nearly finished the last of her large-item sorting for the movers to pack and ship. She was going to send a few of her favorite things from her home over to Rolf's, since it looked like she would be there a while. They were pieces that if she was gone for a long time, she would miss them: the desk that her father had bought her, a rocking horse ornament that Jacob had carved for her, a few pieces from Rolf's childhood that she thought Shaye might want to see.

It had been lovely getting to know her new daughter. Emma didn't understand how Shaye's parents could have just rid themselves of such a sweet girl. Emma was thankful that their mating seemed to be going well. Shaye was now frequently sending Emma texts and pictures from their lives. Rolfston was great at calling his mother and keeping in touch, either by phone or telepathy, but horrible about sending pictures. One of her favorite ones was of the friends hanging out in the backyard. All you could see of the boys were some feet poking out of the top of the hammocks. It did look like a very peaceful place to relax, and she couldn't wait to try it when she got there.

Her phone rang in the kitchen, and she ran to get it. It stopped just as she reached for it. Before she had a chance to check who had called, it started ringing again. It looked like Shaye's number.

"Shaye? Is everything alright?" Emma asked worriedly. Normally, the kids would just leave a voicemail if she did not answer or would check in telepathically to make sure she was okay.

"Emma? It's Tess."

"What happened?" Emma demanded, frantic now that she knew it was not her daughter or son calling from their phone.

"Vlad. The son of a bitch poisoned Rolf's blood. I think we managed to get him stable, but both he and Shaye are unconscious at the moment. She's fine, just overexerted herself trying to heal him. Everyone is here, including Doc who managed to get some charcoal into Rolf to help soak up the poison in his system."

Emma sat on the floor with a thud, her legs giving out from under her. Her visions had not shown her any of this. She was vaguely aware of Samantha coming into the room, sitting next to her, holding her up.

"Do you need me to come? What can I do? What did Doc say, will Rolf be alright?"

"We are taking turns watching over Rolf. I promise we are doing everything we can. Once Shaye wakes up, I am sure she will do another healing session on him. I am holding on to my faith that we can get him through this. Doc is amazing at his job and will not leave until Rolf is on the mend. I know you don't want to hear it but stay there. One of us will keep you updated, I promise. This is just the first break we have had since it happened, and with Shaye passed out, I wanted to call and let you know what is going on. If you cannot reach Rolf telepathically, don't be alarmed. He's been unresponsive to Shaye too. Their bond is still there, he is still alive. Either he is so far under that he cannot communicate even through the bond, or he closed all his links down to keep everything to himself.

"I really hate to dump this on you and run, but I need to get some sleep. I am the only other nurse here besides Shaye to help Doc. One of us will call you later today. I am sending you everyone's phone numbers," Tess added. "Are you going to be okay? Do you have a friend who can stay with you?"

"Samantha is here," Emma responded dully. She was in shock.

"Good. I am falling asleep standing up, so I'm going to go. He is stable right now, I swear. Night, Emma," Tess responded before clicking off.

Emma sat there. Her son was dying. Again. Why couldn't the asshole leave them alone. Pressing a hand to her mouth, she tried to keep the sobs in, but she felt the tears falling anyway. Samantha pulled her into a hug and Emma gave in, her wails deep and painful. Several minutes passed before they calmed into a few tears falling, her breath still hiccupping as she sat up.

"What happened?" Samantha asked, concerned.

"Vlad attacked Rolfston again. This time he poisoned his blood supply. I do not have all the details yet, it just happened today. Tess said they got him stable for the moment, but Shaye passed out after healing him. He was still unconscious. They don't want me coming there," she replied, breath hiccupping as she tried to keep the tears from coming back.

"They are focused on getting Rolfston better. It is not that they don't want you there, it's that they do not want their attention divided between helping Rolfston and keeping your arrival safe."

"My visions did not show me this," Emma said angrily. "They showed me at the battle with Rolfston and his friends. I know we will win, but why did they not show me this?"

"Think, Emma. What did you just say? You saw a future

with Rolfston alive and well enough to fight his father. You already know the outcome. Maybe Fate wanted you to stay here longer and if you had seen Rolfston ill, you would have left too soon."

"Maybe," Emma replied grudgingly. She still thought it was stupid.

"Besides, I may have something for you to use during your battle," Samantha said slyly.

"Hmm?" Emma murmured, laying her head on Samantha's shoulder, her head now pulsing in a dull throb from crying so hard.

"I will have Douglas bring it over," Samantha replied with a mischievous smirk, not giving Emma any clues.

It turned out to be a set of weapons, a sword and dagger that had been forged in dragon's fire and blessed. "These will kill him for sure," Samantha told her.

"These are incredible, but I cannot take such special pieces," Emma protested. She knew what an incredible gift these were. Dragons were reluctant to create such weapons unless they personally knew the wielder. Dragon-forged weapons were much sought after and became family heirlooms, guarded like the greatest treasure.

"You saved my mate, gave us a home and a safe place to raise our family, and welcomed our children to stay on your land. These are a thank-you for your friendship," Douglas told her solemnly. "One of my brothers-in-law is a dragon and we asked him to make these. I know that you don't have the same strength as other vampires, but these should be the perfect weight for your size. The blades are extremely strong and sharp due to the dragon firing process. If we are not going to be close enough to help, we wanted you to have something to protect yourself."

Emma felt her eyes tearing up. She pulled them both into a hug. "Thank you both so much. This is your home for as long as you want to be here, I promise."

❦

"Hey, Mom," her son answered his phone. He had just woken up yesterday from recovering from the poisoning. Shaye had been great about keeping her in the loop.

"Hello, my favorite son. How is everyone doing? How are you feeling?" Her anxiety had been high. Emma kept having visions of the battle, but it all looked like they would be victorious. She was just anxious to reach the time when she would be able to hug her son in person again.

"I am your only son," Rolf responded wryly. "I'm feeling better, everyone is doing okay, Shaye has agreed to turn. She wants to be stronger. I am relieved because she won't be as vulnerable if Vlad attacks again. We have a plan in place to take the fight to him. I'm tired of being surprised by his attacks and only being on the defensive."

"What is the plan?"

As Rolf outlined their strategy for drawing Vlad into a trap, her vision grayed out. She was there! Scenes of being in America, meeting her new expanded family, standing on the battlegrounds, celebrating their victory. It was similar to the vision she already had, but this one lasted a little longer and confirmed their win over Vlad.

"Mom?" Rolf asked, his voice worried.

"Sorry, vision. I am coming. How long do I have to pack up and get there?" She was already darn near ready to go, she just had to finish booking the flight and have the movers get the last of the shipment ready.

"What? What do you mean pack? You are coming here?" Rolf asked, confused.

"I am coming there," she confirmed. "Do you have room for one more? I can find a house nearby if you don't want your mom living with you after all this time. I don't want to cramp your style," she teased, knowing he was probably on the other end of the line wincing at that phrase.

"Are you sure, Mom? Vlad's close. I really do not want him near you."

"I am coming," Emma responded firmly. "Now, where am I staying?"

"There is always room for you here. I'm sure Shaye would love to see you. It's about time she had a caring mom in her life," Rolf told her. "Right now, the plan is set for a couple of weeks out. We want enough time to get Shaye turned and used to her new abilities. There are a few friends that are traveling in to help us as well."

"I cannot wait to meet my new daughter. I will give her all the mom hugs she could want," Emma promised. "The caretakers are going to maintain my house and I'll leave most of my things here, but is it alright if I ship a few things over? There are some things I don't want to be without."

"The circumstances suck, but I am glad I get to see you in person soon. This is your home too, send whatever you want over. I'll order a bed for your room so it will be ready when you come."

After getting off the phone with Rolf, Emma walked out to the small cemetery and sat on the ground. "It is time for me to go away, Jacob. I am going to help my son get rid of Vlad once and for all. I do think it's a little ironic that all those gold coins he used to shame me have been sold to help pay to keep this house and for me to move to America to help defeat him.

"Shaye is simply the perfect mate for Rolf. I cannot wait to see her. I will be sad to be away from you, but Samantha and Douglas will watch over you and the house. I think I'm going to stay in America for a while, but I am keeping this land and will come back to visit. I'll still talk to you while I'm gone, don't worry." She had no idea if her friend could hear her in the afterlife, but if he could, she did not want him to be lonely or to think she had forgotten him. She placed a kiss on the stone marker before rising and saying goodbye to her parents as well.

Emma spent the rest of the day finalizing and arranging her move. It was not the first time she had leased out the house or had it maintained while she was gone. She knew that Samantha and Douglas would take good care of everything. Most of her belongings had already been prepared for shipment and the container would be sent later this week. She had thought that this would be a temporary move, but something was telling her it might be much longer than that. Now she was left wondering how much stuff she should keep here and how much she should try to squeeze into the shipping container. She would bring Rolf's childhood pictures, her journal, and her portrait with Jacob in her carry-on. They had laughed so hard when they had it painted, knowing it was a joke since they weren't really betrothed, but now she treasured it. At this point, she was the only person who remembered him. Rolfston might have a few vague memories, but he had not known Jacob for long.

A little while later, Emma glanced down at her phone as it dinged. It was another update from Shaye. She stood, shaking out the stiffness from sitting on the floor for so long. She had been finding a few family heirlooms from her parents that she would like to bring with her, and a few that she wanted to gift to Samantha and Douglas.

SHAYE: Your son makes the worst patient. He keeps trying to teleport around the house, claiming it uses less energy than walking.

Emma laughed at the picture of her son sleeping on the couch. He was tilted at an odd angle, clearly having fallen asleep while sitting up. There was just the tiniest bit of drool escaping the corner of his mouth.

ME: I would like to say it was because he is a vampire, but he was the same way as a child. He would constantly be trying to sneak out of his bed, even with a fever or sniffles.

SHAYE: So there's no hope then? He is doing much better though. I can't find any trace of the poisons in his system. I think he should be back to normal tomorrow or the day after. Just in time for Halloween. Tess and I are going to drag the guys to a pumpkin patch. We had talked about going before the poison situation. Now I think we definitely need something fun after the past couple of weeks.

ME: We don't get a lot of trick-or-treaters around here, maybe a handful. I'll send you a picture of the turnips we carve. I think Samantha will take her youngest out guising.

SHAYE: Turnips? Guising? What?!

ME: Samantha celebrates Samhain, the old-world holiday Halloween came from. Scotland traditionally carves turnips instead of pumpkins, although the pumpkins are getting popular since they are much easier to carve. Guising is where the children dress up in disguise as evil spirits and go door to door. They must perform a song, a trick, or tell a joke to earn a treat for helping to ward off evil.

SHAYE: Huh. I guess that's where "trick or treat" came from? I don't think we have any turnips big enough to carve, so I guess the guys are stuck with pumpkins. I would love to see the pictures. I'll send you some too. Tess is going to make it a pumpkin carving contest, so it should be fun. We ordered a bunch of decorations to put up.

ME: We don't do much in way of decorations, normally just the carved turnips and pumpkins, a bonfire.

ME: Your birthday is coming up too. I sent a package; I hope it gets there in time. Are you doing anything?

SHAYE: I think everyone is planning something. They're not as sneaky as they think they are. Thank you for thinking of me! I'm sure I'll love it.

ME: I am sure it will be fun, whatever it is.

Emma knew darn well that Rolf had been sitting on a ring for a while now. She had a feeling that he was waiting until Shaye's birthday to ask her. She thought it was sweet that her son was honoring both the paranormal and the human traditions, especially since Shaye was still human.

SHAYE: I better go, he's starting to wake up. I'll make sure to send pictures!

3

Emma had waited long enough. She felt the need to be close to her son, even though she had days before she was supposed to be in America. She called the airlines and was miraculously able to change her flight to tomorrow. She would see her child soon. It had been too long.

The flight and the cab ride seemed to take forever. She was anxious, but mostly excited to see everyone. She paid the driver at the gate and walked up to the house, pulling her extra-large suitcase. Ringing the bell, she waited a couple of minutes until her son opened the door. He just stared at her, speechless.

"Are you going to let me in?" she asked, looking up at him. "It's a little chilly out here."

"Mother, what are you doing here? I thought you weren't coming for another couple of days?" Rolf sounded confused.

"I couldn't wait. I'm so excited to meet her!" Emma practically bounced on her toes, she was so excited. "Where's my hug? Aren't you glad to see me?"

"Yes, of course I'm glad to see you! I was just surprised," he said as he picked her up in a hug.

Emma laughed and squeezed her son tight. "Now put me

down before anyone sees me being silly." It was her first time meeting her son's group in person. She wanted to make a good impression.

"We're all a little silly around here," her son's friend Berkley said, walking up to them. "Sam's pulling Shaye's car into the garage."

"Let's head inside, Mom, and we can talk."

After shutting the door, Rolf walked around the room, making sure the curtains were drawn. "What's going on?" Emma asked.

"Shaye hasn't woken up yet. Tess went into work pretending to be Shaye just in case Vlad has someone watching the clinic. We're trying to keep to the original plan."

"Did I mess up by coming early?" Emma questioned worriedly.

"No, Rolf could use someone to pace with during the day while we're at work," Tess teased as she came into the room. "I'm going to go change and I'll come back to start on dinner."

"I put a white chicken chili in the slow cooker this morning," Rolf said. "It should be ready whenever we want to eat."

"I can go make corn muffins to go with it," Emma offered, feeling bad that she had come early and wanted to help. She walked into the kitchen; she already knew where most everything was from previous video calls with Rolf. He did have such a nice kitchen to cook in.

Once the muffins were in the oven, she set a timer and went into the living room. She could smell a faint hint of the most wonderful scent but could not tell where it was coming from. It made her teeth want to bite something, which was a new experience. She had never been a big fan of drinking from someone. She had been very happy when she was able to get access to blood bags. She looked over the room but didn't see anything that would have such a nice rich smell. It was driving her mad; she normally did not smell scents much better than when she had been human, but this one was sticking out.

When Rolf came back downstairs, she ran over to him. "Rolf, can I talk to you a minute?" she asked, a little frantic. The inability to find the scent was maddening.

"Is everything okay? What's wrong?"

'*Do you smell that?*' she asked, speaking telepathically.

'*I don't smell anything different here, other than dinner,*' Rolf answered, confused. He took a deep breath.

'*Mom, I don't know what you smell. I don't sense anything different,*' he said.

'*It's faint, but I smelled it in here. I just haven't figured out where it's coming from,*' Emma replied.

'*Let's take a walk around the room then and try to figure it out. I'll see if I notice anything different.*'

When they reached the front door, she stopped abruptly by the chair. "Here!" she said excitedly.

"Mom, there's nothing here but Doc's coat. Oh… You haven't met Dr. T yet, have you?" Rolf asked. "He owns a clinic in town and treats humans and paranormals. Shaye works there as a nurse. He's been here forever, but I'm still not sure what kind of paranormal he is. Doc is a great guy," he encouraged her.

"Rolfston, while I'm glad you like your doctor, I'm not sure what that has to do with the smell." Emma was getting frustrated.

"Mom. Think. You noticed one smell above all the others here…" He tried to lead her to the answer.

"Crap." Emma sighed. "I have a mate?" She switched back to speaking mentally. '*I never wanted a mate after your father. You know I get skittish around men sometimes. Maybe I can leave until he goes home, and I can come meet Shaye later?*' she asked hopefully.

'If it were me, what would you tell me, Mom?' Rolf asked, giving her a look.

'To trust in Fate and give him a chance,' she grumbled. When did her kid start listening to her and why did he have to throw it back in her face?

"Exactly. He really is a good guy. I'm pleased with who Fate picked for you. Now, just remember to give him a chance," her son ordered as he turned toward the stairs.

"Hey, Doc. Have you met my mother yet?" Rolf asked, oh so innocently, as a handsome man came into the room. She looked at the man Fate had picked out for her. His lightly tanned skin enhanced the shock of white hair, although she did not think the white was necessarily from age. He looked around her age, maybe a little younger, with only a few laugh lines around his eyes. His eyes were a dark brown, almost black in color, but were kind.

"No, I have not had the pleasure," Doc replied, coming over to shake Emma's hand. He froze as soon as their hands touched. "Mate?" he asked softly.

"Mate," Emma confirmed shakily. "I need to take it slowly though," she admitted. Her hands were trembling just from being near him.

"That is perfectly acceptable. I would love a chance to court you," Doc replied. "My name is Albert."

"Emmaline, but I usually go by Emma," she replied as Doc kissed the back of her hand.

"Hey, what did I miss?" Tess exclaimed, running down the stairs and sliding into the room.

"Shaye is healthy, still sleeping. Mom and Doc are mates," Rolf responded, grinning.

Tess's squeal brought Sam and Berkley out from the kitchen. "Congratulations," they told the newly discovered couple.

"The muffins are done," Berkley added, noticing Emma

could use a break from the attention. "If everyone wants to sit, I can start bringing things out."

Doc looked down at his mate. She was a little shorter than Shaye, closer to Tess's height. He had probably nine inches of height on her. Her inky black hair was pulled into a ponytail, tight curls falling down to brush her shoulders. She had the same piercing blue eyes that her son did, although hers were full of wariness and a bit of fear. He meant it when he said he would love to court her; he would go slowly and show her that she could trust him. He had been waiting so long for his mate, he would not mess it up by rushing her. Doc had heard snippets of conversations from Rolf and his friends. He had heard enough to know that Emma had been hurt in the past.

"You must be hungry from traveling. May I escort you to dinner?" Doc asked, holding out his arm. His skin tingled where she lightly placed her hand. Reaching the table, he pulled out the chair for her.

Doc sat across from Emma. He wanted to be close enough to see and talk to her, but not so close that he would make her nervous. The chicken chili was delightful, something he hadn't had before. It was a nice mix of spice and creaminess from the cheese and sour cream that had been on top.

"Something smells good," they heard someone say. "Is there still some left?" Everyone gasped and turned around to see Shaye standing in the doorway.

"You're awake!" Rolf rushed toward her. He lifted his mate into his arms, holding her tight, his face buried in her neck. Everyone went to hide in the kitchen to give them some privacy. Well, as much privacy as you can have with a group of paranormals with enhanced hearing.

"Mom, come meet my mate, Shaye," Rolf called out.

"Hi, Emma. It's nice to finally meet you," Shaye said.

"Shaye, let me give you a hug. I am so excited to meet my new daughter," Emma said, making sure to give her the best mom hug she could. Both of them had tears in their eyes when the hug ended.

Emma watched as each person took their turn hugging her son's mate. This was such a good group of kids. They really cared about each other. It was nice to see that her son had found himself a good family.

"Are you hungry?" Doc asked after his own hug.

"The chili smells great. I would love a corn muffin," Shaye said, looking toward the kitchen. "You guys go back to eating, I don't want to interrupt. I'll come join you in a minute."

"I meant more like blood," Doc clarified. "Do we smell tasty?" he inquired, lightly teasing. Shaye had already been standing there several minutes and had gotten hugs from everyone in the group. At least one of them should have smelled slightly enticing. He was thrilled Shaye had come through the transition easily, other than sleeping for a long time, but he wanted to make sure she didn't get too thirsty and attack anyone in the group. She would feel horrible if that happened. He was also feeling very protective of his newly found mate.

"Oh! I guess? I mean, I am, but it's not like I can't wait. I can have some with dinner, right? Is it weird that I'm not thirstier?" Shaye asked, looking concerned.

"I think it makes perfect sense," Emma said, giving her a pat on the arm. "Your body knows it can feed safely from its mate, who is right here, so it's not desperate to hunt and feed. You're in your home with your family, so you know you're safe. Plus, you are a healer, so to cause someone an injury by attacking them for food, is to go against your base nature."

Doc thought Emma might be right. Shaye had dedicated her life to helping others. Hurting someone was definitely not her first instinct.

"Sit," Rolf urged Shaye. "I'll go get your dinner and drink."

Shaye sat, looking a little self-conscious with all the attention on her.

"Here you go, love." Rolf kissed the top of her head as he placed her food down in front of her.

Shaye dug into the chili. Doc surreptitiously watched his young charge. He did not want to make her feel more self-conscious, but he wanted to make sure she was getting the right nutrition. After all, she hadn't eaten in several days, so she needed the food and she also needed to drink some blood to satisfy her new physiology. Once she finished the first bowl, Rolf went into the kitchen and came back with another serving. Doc saw Shaye look uncertainly at her mug and then at her mate. Everyone became engrossed in eating their own food and restarting conversations, trying to give Shaye a little privacy to try her new beverage. Doc felt a measure of relief when Shaye finished all her meal. It was rare, but there had been cases of newly turned vampires refusing to drink blood. They had eventually perished.

Once Shaye finished her drink, Rolf stood up and held out his hand to Shaye. "Well, thank you all for coming to dinner. Shaye is getting tired, so I'm going to take her up to bed."

Shaye laughed at her mate but stood and took his hand.

Everyone at the table said goodnight, trying not to smile. Tess waggled her eyebrows at Shaye, humming "Let's Get It On," causing everyone to laugh despite their best efforts to keep a straight face. Doc felt younger being around these people. He thought he might have finally found his tribe. It had been a long time since he had been part of a family group. With his mate here, he was feeling pretty darn content.

This morning had been eventful for so many reasons. Shaye's friend Ian had arrived and had brought with him weapons and armor. When Ian had come into the house, they discovered he was Berkley's mate. The entire group was thrilled for them. After unloading his trailer, Ian had gone upstairs with Berkley to explore their new bond and learn about each other.

'Things are so much better now, Jacob. Not perfect by any means, but it is getting better. I wish you could be here to see it,' Emma thought to her friend. She often wondered what sort of man Jacob would have ended up with. They had talked about it often. Jacob did not think he would find anyone. Emma had been convinced there was someone out there for him; he was handsome and so caring that he would make anyone an amazing partner. Whenever they daydreamed about the future, she told him that they could get married to keep up appearances for the town and that Jacob and his lover could live with her on the farm. They would just say that his man was a farmhand. It would be safe for them in the house to be who they were. Emma certainly never wanted to marry, so pretending to be Jacob's wife and helping her friend would have made her happy.

Bringing herself back to the present, Emma worked alongside her mate to help him get a variety of medical supplies organized for the next day. She had put the multiple slow cookers to use and had dinner cooking. Hopefully the roasts would turn out well. She made a few different types of sandwiches for lunch, with Albert helping make a coleslaw and a fruit salad. Placing everything on the table, she poked her head out of the kitchen.

"Why don't you all come and eat?" Emma said. "I'll save some for Ian and Berkley when they come down."

She was nervous about tomorrow and staying busy was helping. The thought of seeing Vlad again was slightly terrifying. It had taken her years to even leave her property after the first attack. Even now, she still had days where her anxiety was high, and it would take her a while to work up the nerve to leave the safety of the grounds. It had been worse when Vlad had been in the same country and had still been taunting her. When Rolf turned her, it at least gave her the ability to hold her own a little better against Vlad. Choosing to see him and potentially fight against him, had her anxiety skyrocketing. Emma kept reminding herself that she wouldn't be alone with him this time. She had a whole family of paranormals surrounding her. Not to mention that Samantha and Douglas had generously gifted her with dragon-forged weapons. She made a mental note to call them after the battle and check in.

It was a beautiful day for a commitment ceremony. The sun shone bright, and the skies were clear just like in her vision. Everyone was spending a little more quality time with their significant others before it was showtime. She was still wary around Albert, even though she knew Fate would not give her an abusive mate and the whole group here seemed to love him. Her heart felt better when she was near him, her anxiety calmed, so she helped him go over the medical supplies one last time. Emma put the slow cookers to use again making soups for dinner. Everyone would be hungry after the battle and having a pizza delivery with potential bloodshed in the yard didn't seem like a great idea. Shaye and Tess had made rolls last night to go with the soups. Emma tried to take comfort in the fact that her visions had not changed; she still saw them being victorious today.

When the time came, she began to walk to the platform with Shaye and Tess. She thought Shaye looked beautiful in an off-white knee-length Renaissance-style dress with a loose, flowing skirt that was slightly longer in the back. The sleeves were also loose and reached down to her wrists. The black battle armor that Ian had made for her looked like a bodice or corset, emphasizing her waist. Her wavy brown hair was down, save for a braid on either side that formed a crown.

The pendant from Berkley was prominently displayed and already glowing, alerting everyone that there was danger nearby. Emma tried searching the crowd without being too obvious.

Once they reached the platform, Emma took the last few steps to stand in her place in front. "Thank you, everyone, for coming to see my only son, Rolfston, and my new daughter-in-law Shaye's Mating Ceremony. I am so excited for her to join our family. As you may know, she helped save Rolfston's life twice recently. We are pleased that she has decided to not only join with Rolfston in the mating ceremony, but also through turning. Our paranormal family will grow tonight, and I personally think she is going to be a great addition."

"I don't think so, Emmaline," a new voice sneered. Everyone turned around to stare at the man standing at the back of the group. The monster had arrived. It was predictable, but still terrifying.

Rolf moved to stand slightly in front of her, Shaye, and Tess as he confronted his father. Emma kept one hand on her dagger. Her fragile mate bond with Albert told her that he had come out further onto the patio. She took comfort in the fact that he would help look after them.

With his enhanced hearing, Doc stood in the shadows near the house and listened to Rolf and Vlad's conversation. Rolf was a good man, he thought. Even now, Rolf was trying to avoid bloodshed and give his father one last chance. Doc knew it was a hopeless effort, Vlad was too far gone into madness to be reached. He stood ready and watched over his new family, prepared to jump into the fight if he was needed. Doc had waited decades to find his tribe, and nothing would take them from him. Although he had not anticipated having an adult stepson, he thought wryly. His beast urged him to pay attention as he heard the first slide of metal against a scabbard.

As the battle raged, he was relieved to see that their side

was the strongest. Doc kept a close eye on his people. Looking around, Gawain caught his attention. He was in falcon form, flying high. Doc was unsure why he chose that over human. As Gawain plunged down toward one of Vlad's minions, a vampire grabbed his talons and threw him toward someone's sword. Doc gestured and managed to control enough air to move Gawain out of the path of the sword. Unfortunately, he did not have enough time to plan where to direct Gawain. Doc winced as Gawain hit a tree; he would probably have a concussion, but it was better than being impaled. As a few injured started making their way to the patio, Doc's attention was pulled between the battle and the need to heal.

There was an almost palpable sense of a climax to the battle. He turned and watched as Rolf and Shaye worked together to kill Vlad. Shaye managed to stab Vlad in the stomach, Rolf stabbed him in the heart, twisting the blade to destroy it. His mate walked over to the body, her weapons drawn. Doc desperately wanted to go over to her but knew that she needed to do this on her own. After years of fear, she needed the closure.

"We better make sure the bastard is really dead," Emma muttered to herself. Destroying the heart, dismemberment, and fire were the only ways that she knew of to make sure the monster stayed dead. She stood over his body, giving it a kick as she cursed at him. "Piece of shit, son of a bitch. Taking things from other people that weren't yours. Hurting people just for your own pleasure. Taking my baby from me, trying to turn him to be like you, then trying to kill him when he was a good soul. Never again. We're making sure you can't hurt anyone else," Emma vowed. She knelt next to the body and used her dagger to cut out the remains of his heart. Standing, she dropped it next to his body before swinging her sword as hard as she could to decapitate the head. Her family watched as she proceeded to use her blades to remove each of his limbs. "Maybe some fire as well," she murmured, looking around. She wanted to ensure that there was no way his minions could piece him back together. "Hey, you! Dragon! Can you burn this for me?" Emma asked.

"Mom, are you alright?" Rolf asked, concerned.

"Yes, just making sure the asshole can't come back," Emma replied calmly, panting a bit from the exertion. She was grateful for the dragon-forged blades; she'd have to tell Douglas and Samantha that they had worked wonderfully. She would not have been able to dismember him otherwise.

The dragon landed. "If you get all the bodies together, I can burn them all at once."

"Let me check with the Sheriff first. I'm not sure if we're supposed to follow any certain Warden rules for this," Rolf replied. He stepped off to the side to make the phone call.

The Sheriff arrived quickly, and Emma moved off to the side. He was a huge man, both in presence and physical size; he was intimidating. Once he finished whatever Warden things he needed, he let the dragon set fire to the pile of bodies. Berkley was smart and quickly created a dome around the pyre to contain the flames and the smell.

Her mate bond was screaming at her. She could sense just how much Albert wanted to come and comfort her, but she knew he was trying to give her the space and time that she needed. Emma walked over to her mate and let him hold her as she watched the flames. "It's over now," she said in relief. "He can't hurt us anymore."

Once everything had burned down to ashes, Emma took a step back and gave Doc a kiss on the cheek. "I'm going to go bring the food out. Everyone is going to need the energy after fighting." Her stomach roiled and she didn't think she would be able to eat. It wasn't just the fact that Vlad had shown up, but that she was also surrounded by so many new people. Despite that, she felt lighter somehow. The knowledge that there would not be a voice whispering creepily in her ear as she walked through town, that there would not be any more coins on her doorstep, made her feel free.

Shaye followed her in and between the two of them, it only took a few trips to bring out the food. They placed everything on a table by the house; food, bowls, spoons, and the baskets filled with bread and butter. There were a few coolers around the patio containing drinks. Once everyone had eaten, they could find places for people to sleep if they wanted to stay.

It had been a week since Vlad had been dispensed. Emma had received the shipping container with her belongings and had finally gotten her room set up the way she wanted it. It was great that there were so many people around the house to help her carry things upstairs. She loved her room; it was a pale blue and very calming. There was a nice view out her windows, and she loved sitting at her desk and watching creatures that would stroll through the yard. In addition to moving in, she and the girls had also come up with a dinner plan for Thanksgiving.

Today though, everyone was relaxing. Rolf and Shaye were reading in the library. Ian and Berkley were sketching out some kind of design. Albert was reading a medical journal on the couch. He had been coming by daily to see her; sometimes they talked, sometimes they took a stroll around the yard, and sometimes he just hung out in the house, letting her get used to his presence. After living by herself for so long, it was an adjustment living with several other people. Samantha and Douglas had lived in a separate house on the property, so she had never really run into anyone unexpectedly while walking around her home.

Emma was in the kitchen working on a new brownie recipe using peanut butter. Tess was experimenting with different autumn-themed cookie recipes. One of them was a pumpkin cookie with a cream cheese filling. Emma was eager to try that one once it cooled. Tess had warned her not to call it Pumpkin Spice anything, as Shaye had a hate relationship with the overabundance of Pumpkin Spiced snacks during the fall. This was closer to a pumpkin roll or pumpkin cake, so Tess thought Shaye would like it. Sam kept stealing cookies when Tess wasn't looking and was trying to take a nibble out of the brownies as well. Emma just laughed and shook her head at him. She really enjoyed being part of this group. They were fun to be around.

Rolf came into the living room and cleared his throat. "What does everyone think about me declaring us officially a Clan? We'd keep it here on the house and grounds. It would be inclusive since we are all different species. If someone new wanted to join, the eight of us would all have input on if they were accepted. You guys would be the Clan Council. If you want to live outside of this house, we can build on the property for whatever you want. We're already looking at building a forge and kiln area for Ian and Berkley, if they can decide on a design."

Berkley spoke up. "We're all in. We talked about it, and we would love to officially be a family, a Clan." Everyone nodded their agreement. Both Tess and Emma had brought it up to the group as a possibility, since they had both had visions about it.

Rolf sighed in relief. "Great, I'll get the paperwork started today."

"What is the name of the Clan?" Emma asked.

"Welcome, everyone, to the Nightwood Clan," Rolf announced.

4

Doc sat in his office between patients. His mate was on his mind. He promised to give her time, and he would. It was harder than he thought it would be not to be near her, especially when his animal side pushed hard. It was part of the reason he had started coming over to the Clan house after work. It was great to see all the kids and not spend all his non-working time alone. After a thousand years, he had a family. Well, he supposed it was really only five to eight hundred years alone, give or take a couple of hundred. He had lost count along the way. He had always been a little bit of a loner, more due to circumstances than desire, and he was surprised how much he wanted to be near this specific group of people. He had traveled the world, learned so much, made friends here and there, but until he came to Rockfort, he had never settled down for long. He had been here about two hundred years working as the town's doctor. He had dyed his hair black when he first got to town and then slowly let the white creep back in to help show his age. Then he would vacation for a few weeks to a month out of town, come back with it dyed black again and start over as his own nephew, son, etcetera. Doc had been so relieved when the townspeople seemed to accept the paranormals that lived there. It meant that he could stop dying his hair.

There was a knock on the door a few seconds before Shaye stuck her head in.

"Are you busy?" she asked.

He shook his head. "Come on in. I'm just woolgathering."

"How are you?"

"I'm fine. Why do you ask?" Doc thought he had been covering up his longing pretty well.

Shaye gave him a long look. "I can sense it. Ever since you started hanging out with us more, I can get a sense of your well-being. I can feel that you are struggling. I wanted to let you know that Emma does feel drawn to you, the mate bond is helping. Just keep showing her what a good guy you are. She may need some patience, but Tess says she will get there. I just wanted to let you know not to give up hope," Shaye tried to reassure him. "By the way, Emma loves the wild-flower type of flowers," she added with a wink as she shut the door on her way out.

Doc sat back in his seat, thinking. His garden had stopped blooming, but maybe the local flower shop would have something. He wanted to make sure she knew he was thinking of her without being overwhelming, so maybe he could get the flowers delivered.

Picking up the phone, he called the florist.

"Good morning, thank you for calling Rockfort Blooms. How may I help you?" A cheerful voice answered.

"Morning, Beth. I need to get an order of wildflowers delivered today. Do you have any in stock?" Doc asked.

"Sure do. Who are they for?"

"Emma," Doc replied.

"Get your butt over here and pick out your own flowers for your lady," Beth scolded. "It will mean more if you pick them out. Plus, you can sign a card that way. Come over when you get a break. I will set some off to the side to make sure I don't run out, but you should create the bouquet yourself."

Doc stared at the phone, listening to the dial tone as Beth hung up on him. Standing up, he walked over to the door and strolled down to the front desk.

"Sherri, do I have any open time today?"

Sherri hummed, looking through the computer for the day's calendar. "It looks like you have an hour and a half at lunch from eleven o'clock until twelve thirty. Do you want me to make sure that time stays clear?"

"Yes, please. I am going to run next door to pick out some flowers for Emma. Why don't I grab lunch on my way back? Close the office for that time and we can all have a nice lunch break," Doc suggested.

Shaye came out of an exam room with the medical file. "Wellness visit, Doc. Robbie just turned four, so he is due for some vaccinations. I can place the lunch order with Sam, if you let me know what you want," Shaye offered.

"I'll take the steak salad with Ranch dressing. Just let Sam know it is for me; he adds in extra vegetables," Doc replied. He did love his vegetables; of course, that was probably due to his animal side, but they were tasty regardless.

"Will do," Shaye replied before handing the folder to Doc. As she handed it to him, she made sure to touch his hand, sending some calm healing vibes his way.

"Thank you," he told her with a small smile. Doc counted himself very lucky that he had such a great staff. Shaye and her group felt like his family. Every day he got to know them better and had started seeing them more as his kids, not just some people he knew. He knew they were all adults, some of them two hundred years old, but he was still older. Plus, it was in his nature to be a caregiver, hence why he became a doctor.

Feeling his tension dissipate, he took a deep breath before opening the exam room door. "Good morning, Robbie! I think you have grown! Are you almost as tall as me now?" Doc joked as he walked into the room.

As the morning continued, he found himself both eager and anxious to go to the florist. He could not wait to find something that would make Emma smile, but at the same time he and his animal were fighting. His animal was a pushy bastard and did not understand why they couldn't be near their mate all the time. It didn't help that he and his animal were more like separate entities than most shifters. Even after all this time, he didn't really understand it. Shifters were the same person whether they were animal or human; the two forms didn't talk to each other necessarily, although if a wolf's senses picked up on danger the human did not, then the wolf might push a sensation at the human side, but it wasn't really communication, more of a subconscious type of thing. He and his animal often felt separate. They were connected, but the animal often had different opinions than he did, and he had to try to reconcile the two sides of himself. It could be exhausting, as was the case now. The human side knew they had to give Emma time to trust him, to accept him as her mate. The animal side thought if they just stood near her all the time, she would want to be with them. *We have to give her space* and *time,'* he thought to his animal. The asshole just huffed at him and pranced off to sulk in the back of his mind.

Doc sighed as he finished up the notes from the last visit. Luckily, it had been mundane things bringing people in lately, mostly well visits or a few early colds. He threw on a light jacket and walked toward the front of the office. "I'm off to the florist and then I will pick up the food at Sam's. I should be back in a half hour to forty-five minutes. Feel free to lock the front door and put up an Out To Lunch sign."

He took a deep breath as he walked outside. His animal enjoyed being out in the fresh air. This town was home after looking for one for so long. As the only doctor not located in the hospital, Doc saw most of the people in town at some point. He loved seeing his patients as he walked around town, watching them grow up and bring kids of their own into the clinic.

The bell dangling over the shop's door dinged as he opened it.

"Morning, Beth. I've come to look at those flowers," Doc said as he walked up to the desk.

"I cannot believe you weren't going to pick them out yourself," she replied, disappointment coloring her tone.

"It's been a long time since I sent someone flowers. It wasn't even on my radar, until Shaye gave me the idea." Doc couldn't think of a time where he sent romantic flowers; they had all been for funerals, congratulations, or for his front desk staff through the years for holidays.

"Are you going to deliver these yourself, or do you still want me to take them over?" Beth questioned.

"I'd love it if they could be delivered. I want her to know I am thinking of her, but I don't want to intrude on her if she is not ready for company."

"Still taking it slow?" Beth asked, curious.

"Yes. She has good reason to be cautious. She needs time to trust me. I would never hurt her, she is my mate, but she needs to come to that knowledge herself, or she will never fully believe it," Doc answered.

Beth looked thoughtful. "Well, I cannot imagine how hard it is to not claim your mate right away. It always seems to happen so fast with paranormals. Josh claimed me in two days," she replied, laughing. Her husband Josh was a witch who had come through town on a business trip about twenty years ago. Once he met Beth, he decided to stay in Rockfort and started his own accounting business. He did the accounting for all the town's businesses and their son had just declared his major to be in accounting so he could join his dad when he graduated. Doc was happy that

Jonathan was going to come back to town when he was finished with college. He had helped Beth bring each of her children into the world. Jonathan was the first one to leave the nest.

"Her experience with men has not been good, and I can wait. It might be a little hard, but I know it's right for our relationship. Feel free to slip in what a good guy I am though," he joked.

"One of the best I know," Beth replied, serious.

Doc felt his cheeks heat at the compliment. He cleared his throat. "Are these the wildflowers?" he asked, changing the subject.

Beth nodded as Doc started picking out the blooms he thought would go well together, something cheery and colorful. The yellows, oranges, and red reminded him of a sunset. He added some purple flowers to give it something different. *Green*, his animal added. Doc mentally shook his head but added a few green leafy items to the bouquet as well.

"Can you send this with a vase? I'm not sure if they have one," Doc asked as he finished completing his gift.

"I can. You want them delivered today? I can add a box of chocolates to go with it, if you would like," Beth offered.

"Yes, please. Dark chocolate if you have any. Maybe a turtle or a caramel…and make sure you give it directly to Emma. Otherwise, the chocolate might disappear." He laughed. "The kids have a sweet tooth."

Beth looked up from tying a bow around the flower vase. "I have to say, Doc, that it is nice to see you happy. I'm glad you finally found your people."

"The whole town is my people," Doc protested. "I care for all of you."

"Yes, you do," Beth agreed. "But these are your group, your clan, your family, your tribe, as it were. I can tell that you feel at home with them, and I am so pleased for you. You deserve to have a group all your own after taking care of all of us for so long." She came around the counter and gave him a hug.

"I will deliver these personally," she promised. "I can shut down for a half hour for lunch and drive over to Rolf's."

"Thank you, Beth," Doc replied, dropping a kiss to her cheek.

Walking down the street to Sam's, he felt peace between himself and his animal for the first time since meeting Emma. They were both pleased with the gift.

He took a deep breath as he entered the brewery. The smell of fries hung in the air and his stomach grumbled. He loved Sam's fries, although he tried not to eat them too often. Even with his shifter metabolism, he wanted to set a good example for his patients. The witches and humans still needed to eat healthy and to take care of themselves. Although, he thought he noticed Shaye subtly helping a few of them with their high cholesterol and other smaller ailments that could cause problems.

"What's up, Doc?" Sam laughed. He never got tired of the Bugs Bunny joke.

He sighed, trying not to smile. It would only encourage him to do it more. "Hi, Sam. I am picking up lunch for the office."

"It's ready. Rolf wanted to know if you were coming to dinner tonight? We were going to keep it relaxed, just grilling, and hanging out with the fireplace on. It looks like it'll be a good evening for sitting outside," Sam offered.

"That sounds good. I would love to come to dinner. Can I bring anything?"

"I think everything is covered, unless there's something special you wanted to have," Sam answered.

"I'm easy. If you guys need anything last minute, just give me a call and I'll grab it on my way."

A server came over to them with a to-go bag. "I threw in some extra napkins and silverware."

"Thank you. I will see you tonight, Sam." Doc took the bag of food and headed back to the office. It would be nice to be able to sit and enjoy lunch with Shaye and Sherri. Dinner tonight with the whole group would make for a very nice day, he thought cheerfully.

Emma took a deep breath, trying to calm her nerves. She had managed to walk down to Albert's all on her own. Her goal had been to make it there and ask if he wanted to take a walk with her, but just leaving the property by herself had been harder than she thought. This was ridiculous, she scolded herself. She was a grown woman who should be able to walk down the street without having this much anxiety. Vlad was gone. Nothing could be much worse than him. Unfortunately, her stomach didn't get that memo. It was roiling, full of stomach acid, making her nauseous. She took several deep breaths to keep from vomiting. She had been so focused on getting to Albert's that she hadn't noticed the problem growing until she stopped outside of the safety of his house.

The last thing she wanted to do was vomit on her mate, so she stood in his yard, hiding behind a tree, waiting for her stomach to get itself under control. She tried to distract herself by finding details about his house that she hadn't noticed before. It was a smart design with the traditional Cape Cod house on the left side and an addition with a wide porch for the clinic off to the right. From where she stood, she could see a Personal Residence plaque by the house doorbell, along with a smaller sign that directed people needing the clinic to the door further to the right. The clinic side was also marked by a sign with the clinic's hours. The landscaping was simple, but welcoming. He even had a picnic table on the clinic's porch. Wandering over to it, she saw a bin underneath labeled toys and another one labeled coloring. Opening the coloring bin, she took out a sheet and some crayons. Her fingers were still trembling; apparently, the pep talk to herself had not worked very well. She gripped a crayon tightly, trying to force her hand to still enough to color. She really should have dug out her adult coloring books at the house. She had started using them as a calming method based on a recommendation from a therapist she had spoken to years ago. Coloring was repetitive enough to send her into a slightly calmer state.

"Emma? Are you alright?" Doc asked, concerned, as he walked out the front door. He sat next to her and gently pressed his fingers to her wrist. She knew her heartbeat was racing, and she still felt a little shaky.

"I'm fine, honestly. I just got a little overwhelmed. I am so sorry; I sat down trying to calm a little bit before ringing the doorbell. I wanted to surprise you and see if you wanted to take a walk with me," Emma explained, a little embarrassed.

"I would love to take a walk. Maybe we can go down to the bookstore and wander around? Let's get you a cup of chamomile tea first, that should help settle you," Doc offered. He was proud of his mate for venturing out of Rolf's house, but worried at the same time. "Do you want to sit out here or come into the kitchen while I get the tea ready?"

"I would love to see the kitchen," Emma answered, packing away the crayons.

She followed Albert inside and down the short hallway to the small kitchen. He had a two-person table against the one wall, a stove/oven, a refrigerator, and a handful of cabinets. It was a tiny space, but she figured it was usually only him there, as she did not smell any other scents. Emma watched as he got the water boiling on the stove and then pulled out a tea pot and cups. It was a beautiful set, a lovely green color, shimmering with silver designs. She watched as Albert measured out some loose tea leaves into a small diffuser, which he placed inside the teapot and then poured the boiling water over.

"That is a beautiful set. What is it made from?" Emma asked, both curious and wanting to fill the silence. Her stomach was finally settling. Being near her mate seemed to help.

"Jade and silver. I have had the set for a long time; it is one of my favorites. Jade is supposed to bring good luck and have healing properties," Doc answered as he allowed the tea to steep for a couple of minutes. It was his oldest teapot, one he had collected on his travels when he was younger. Although he had no scientific proof behind the effects of the jade, he always felt calmer and more at peace after using the teapot. It had been blessed by the person who had given it to him.

"What made you venture out today?" Doc questioned gently.

"I wanted to say thank you again for the flowers and chocolates. I haven't been sent flowers before. Well, besides the ones Rolfston sends me. It was a very nice surprise." Emma blushed as she realized just how sad that sounded. Over two hundred years old and she had never received flowers, other than the ones from her son.

"I will have to make sure you get more of them, then." Doc smiled at his mate. How had no one appreciated this woman before? He would make sure she knew just how special he thought she was.

Emma glanced down at her lap, twisting her fingers together. Albert really was such a nice man, his dark eyes always kind. If she could only get herself to stop being so anxious and to accept him fully as her mate.

"Emmaline. Stop," Doc gently commanded. "Tell me what has you worried. I will try to help." He poured the tea and passed a cup to her, hoping the calming tea and the jade would help.

"I really do want to be your mate. I am just not ready yet.

And I feel awful for making you wait. I can sense your animal getting frustrated sometimes."

"He can be patient. He likes being close to you and the distance sometimes makes him a little antsy. He is *fine*, however. We will take as long as you need. I want you to be comfortable near me, not as an obligation or what you think you should or need to do, but because you want to be. You set the pace. I am just happy knowing you are my mate," Doc replied honestly.

Emma took a sip of her drink. It was the perfect temperature and a nice delicate tea. The cherished jade cup made it feel special.

"I am working on leaving the safety of the house more. I was a little more comfortable doing it back home, but when I moved here, it seems like all my old fears came back up. Right after Vlad, I was afraid to leave the house for the longest time. I got over it then…well, mostly. I will get over it now. Your size is another factor. I am working on that as well. It has nothing to do with you, not really," Emma tried to reassure him.

"I think you are doing very well," Doc praised her. "It had to be scary to leave your home and come to a new country. Fears are often not rational. I am serious about taking this at your speed."

"Do you think we could speak on the phone?" Emma suggested. She was desperate to know her mate but being physically in his presence took a while to get used to. She was hoping that by talking to him over the phone and establishing a bond that way, that she would get over her irrational fears faster. "At night, of course, so I don't interrupt your patients."

"I would like that," Doc replied. Any chance to speak to Emma was a blessing.

Emma finished her tea and set her cup down. "Would you like to go to the bookstore? I was hoping to find a new book to read." She felt much more settled and less anxious after her tea. Maybe the jade really did have some healing properties.

"That sounds delightful. Let me clean this up and we can head over. Would you like to walk or drive over?" Doc asked as he rinsed and dried the cups and teapot.

"It is sunny out, so I was hoping we could walk."

Doc opened the door for his mate. He wanted to offer his arm but didn't think she would be comfortable holding on to him yet. He breathed a sigh of relief when the bookstore was not crowded. He saw Tess sitting at the corner working on her laptop. A familiar face should help Emma feel more comfortable.

"What type of book were you looking for?" Doc asked.

"I wanted to find a new crossword or word search book… and maybe a fun reading book too," Emma said. She could feel a slight blush on her cheeks. She really wanted to find a romance book. The crossword or word search would be entertaining, but what she really wanted was a nice juicy romance.

"Hmm. I think the romances are toward the back of the store," Doc replied. "Do you want to go look at those? I was going to run over to the medical magazines and see if there was anything new." He knew there wasn't. He had subscriptions to a lot of them, but he wanted to give her the space to find a book she would like without being embarrassed he was there.

Emma nodded. "I will just be a few minutes." She knew what he was doing, but she appreciated it all the same.

Emma walked over to the romance section and skimmed the backs of some covers. She found the paranormal romances humorous, as they often got things wrong. She didn't really like the historical romances for the same reason. Maybe something with aliens, she thought as she saw a cover with a blue-skinned man on it. This one looked like it had potential, she thought to herself. There was another one that looked funny, about a psychic and his co-worker. They both looked good, how would she choose? She would pick out a puzzle book and then try to narrow it down, she determined.

Doc watched as his mate tried to decide between two books. She would be getting both books today, he decided. He wanted to do something that would make her smile, and it seemed like that would be an easy way to do it. After she picked out a word search book, he went over to her and took her books.

"I'll go check out, if you are ready?" he asked.

"Oh! I was trying to pick out which of those two I was going to get."

"I am getting you both, that way you don't have to pick," Doc answered. "It is my gift for such a lovely date," he added when he saw she was going to protest.

"Thank you," Emma replied, blushing when she realized Albert would see the covers.

5

Doc was trying to catch up on his laundry when he heard his personal phone ring. Dropping the towel he was holding, he ran into the kitchen to grab it before it stopped. He stabbed at it with his finger, trying to get it to connect.

"Hello?"

"Albert? Did I get you at a bad time?" Emma's quiet voice asked on the other end.

"No. No, I was just in the laundry room folding a basket. I had left my phone in the kitchen earlier and forgot to bring it with me." Doc loved how she was the only one to call him Albert. It made him feel like it was a special name she had just for him, which was a little ridiculous if he thought about it since it was his actual name.

"How was your day?" he asked her. He hadn't seen her in a couple of days, as the clinic had been overwhelmed with the flu and strep throat going around. He was grateful for his shifter side, as he was immune to the germs. He had made it an office policy to wear a face mask though when dealing with people; many of his staff were still vulnerable to germs, and so were many of his patients. There had been a mini baby boom this past month. There were about five deliveries that he had attended, and he could not be happier with how healthy each new little person was. He would do his best to keep them that way.

"It was pretty good. I finished the one book you bought me. Rolf had the outdoor fireplace and hammocks set up, so I sat out there for a little bit. It is a nice spot to read. I think he will have to take the hammocks down soon though; it's getting too cold."

Emma sounded sad that the hammocks would be going away. "Berkley or Tess might be able to create a dome over the back patio. With the fireplace going, it should help keep it a reasonable temperature and keep the snow out," Doc suggested. He grabbed a glass of water and sat down on his couch. He wanted to be able to enjoy his conversation with his mate and focus on her. The laundry could wait a little longer.

"That is a good idea!" Emma exclaimed excitedly. "I will ask them about it. How was your day?"

"It went pretty well. I had a few of the new babies come in for their check-ups. We had a couple new flu and strep cases that popped up. It's been a bad year so far and the season is just getting started."

"I heard! I must say that I do not miss getting all the different ailments that went with being human. I might not be as strong or have as good of senses as the other vampires, but at least I have their immunity to germs.

"Shaye tried a new recipe for dinner; it was a chicken and apple dish with a balsamic vinegar drizzle. She roasted Brussels sprouts as well. Normally I am not a big fan of the tiny cabbage-looking things, but she had some nice seasoning on them, and they were not mushy. I would eat them again," Emma said with a grin. She had enjoyed the dinner, the only thing lacking had been her mate. She had missed him the last couple of days. They had sent texts back and forth, mostly good morning/good night type of things, but had not been able to speak on the phone yet. She took a chance tonight that he would be available to talk.

"That sounds good. I love her Brussels sprouts. I had leftovers from last night's dinner. Nothing exciting, just a chicken soup I threw together in the slow cooker. It turned out decent though. I think I may close the office on Sunday and refer people to the hospital if they need to be seen. I usually only have the clinic open on Sundays for walk-ins anyway. This week has been busy, and I would love to spend time with everyone again. Maybe we could go out on Sunday? Something close to the house, maybe outside if it is nice out?" Doc asked hopefully.

"That sounds like fun. I have missed talking to you this week," Emma confessed.

"What have you been up to?" Doc felt a thrill go through him when he heard she would go on a date with him. He was slowly making progress, he thought.

"A lot of reading. I worked on a new bread recipe with Tess. It was a braided seeded bread. It turned out nice. I am going to try to adjust it a little bit tomorrow and will save some for you. I talked to the caretakers back home and checked on everything there. It seems to be going well. One of their younger girls has a date this weekend, so Douglas is being grumpy." Emma laughed, picturing his face. She had seen it every time one of his children started dating.

"Ah, I imagine that would make one a little grumpy," Doc agreed. He did not have any children of his own, but he felt like the Clan's members were his adopted kids. If they were younger, he would definitely be grumpy about them dating. Especially if it was not their mate; who knew how a non-mate would treat them. "I assume it's not her mate then?"

"No. A local boy from town asked her out. It's harder to find your mate in a small town, so most of the paranormals will date locals at least through high school. It helps everyone fit in. Small towns can be great for lots of things, but if someone does not follow the social norms, they stand out. Usually, they break it off and go to college or leave to find a job in a larger town. Douglas knows this, but it still makes him grumpy."

"That does make sense. It is hard to be the only one standing out in a small group," Doc agreed, thinking back to his younger years. He had been the only shifter of his kind in his tribe. Before everyone shifted for the first time, it had not been an issue and he had plenty of friends to play with. His parents were never great, more of a hands-off parenting style. If there was food available, he had some type of clothing, and was not left behind when they moved, they considered their job done. After he had shifted and was different from everyone else, he had been ostracized by his friends and his parents ignored him even more. The tribe leader did not want him there but couldn't kick him out yet. He was still a minor according to their tribe laws and therefore was supposed to be under the protection of the leader. Luckily, one of the elders took notice and brought him under her wing. Thalia taught him the art of healing and found him any obscure references to his animal that she could find. He still did not know what caused him and his animal to be so different in how they interacted when compared to other shifters. He stayed with the tribe until he reached adulthood and before he left, she had gifted him the materials that she had collected for him, along with some dried meat, some root vegetables since they would last a while, healing supplies, and a few items to trade for things he might need along his journey. Doc had traveled, working as a healer when he could, learning additional remedies from others in the healing arts. He gathered as many old references as possible, trying to understand himself a little better. After many years passed, he ventured back to his tribe's last location. There had been no one. The settlement, as crude as it was, was destroyed. It looked like buildings had broken down from age, not from an attack. He found several marked graves, including his own parents. He had stopped aging, but they had not. He continued researching to this day.

"Albert, are you alright? You sound sad and I can…feel it through the bond," Emma asked, concerned.

"Just remembering. Old hurts, nothing new," he tried to reassure her. "I was the child that stuck out. I did not fit in with our community and was asked to leave as soon as I reached adulthood. Even though this is my home, and I felt the most accepted here, I still felt like a bit of an outsider. The kids have all made me feel welcome at the Clan house and I feel like I finally found my place. The town was part of it, I was just waiting for the rest of them. If that makes sense," Doc tried to explain.

"It does. I felt the same way about my house in England. We moved there after Vlad and while it was safe for me, it wasn't until Jacob came to the farm that it started feeling more like my home. We looked out for each other," Emma told him.

This was the first time she had mentioned a Jacob. He took a quiet breath in and held it. She did have a life before him, which was perfectly reasonable, but he hadn't thought he needed to win her affections over from another man. Emmaline was so nervous around the men in town, he had thought that she was scared of all men. It would crush him if it turned out it was specifically him. He wasn't sure how to proceed with the rest of the conversation now. He did not want to come off as a caveman.

"Is he your betrothed?" He tried to ask casually. If the man lived with her on the farm, he had to be important to her.

"Yes," Emma responded.

"Oh." Doc felt his heart break. He had no desire to break up a relationship, no matter that she was his fated mate. This was his home, but if she moved here permanently, he would need to move. It would be too hard to see her every day knowing she would never be his.

"No! Not like that!" Emma cried out. She could feel Doc's pain along their bond and felt it actually weaken under the pain. "He passed away many years ago…" Emma began but had to take a breath. Between the remembered pain of Jacob's passing and the sensation of Doc's pain, she felt over-whelmed for a moment.

"You do not have to tell me," Doc tried to reassure her. "I can let you go and stop bothering you," he told her with an apology in his voice.

"Stop it right now, you silly man. I just need a minute. You misunderstood," Emma told him, sniffing. The crazy man thought he would give her up. Dumb mate.

"Jacob was a farmhand that we had hired right before Rolf was turned and disappeared with Vlad. Rolf didn't know him very well. We became friends of a sort since we saw each other every day. I had problems leaving the property even then, although when Rolf was home, I felt safer. Vlad had found our new home not long after my parents passed away and would randomly show up, finding ways to let me know he was near. The visits got worse after I was a vampire, but even when I was human it was still enough to make me afraid of leaving the house. Anyway," Emma tried to get back on track with her story. "One night I heard noises outside and took a peek to see what the problem was. I was terrified Vlad had come back, hopeful it was Rolf returning home, worried a fox got into the chicken coop. I saw Jacob and another man kissing. At that time, especially in rural England, that sort of thing was most definitely not accepted. Jacob was terrified I was going to turn him in. His friend ran off, but I told Jacob to come inside the house. I made tea and told him the real story behind Rolf's conception and that the man was still out there and that was why I was so afraid of going into town. We became friends, we hid nothing from each other any longer. Jacob took over many of the chores that had to be run in town or made sure to accompany me, so I wasn't by myself. I told him he was welcome to have any friends over; he kept them close to his cabin though, since I feared other men getting close to me.

"There were whisperings in the town about how I was too stuck up to remarry. Some of the women were especially rude when I tried to sell or barter goods. Jacob and I decided to tell them we were betrothed; it would help protect both of us. I would have been happy to marry him. He was a good friend and protector, and I could protect him too in my own way. Vlad came back one day after Rolf refused to follow in his footsteps. He wanted to try again for a successor, or right-hand man, I'm not sure. I was the only one that had birthed a child for him that had been successfully turned into a vampire. Jacob returned and stopped him before he could... He wouldn't run when I told him to, and Vlad killed him. Rolf came back just in time to turn me and save me," Emma ended on a sob.

"Oh, love. I am so sorry you lost your friend. And I am sorry I misunderstood." Doc felt horrible that he made her relive that to appease his bruised ego.

Emma quietly blew her nose. "Stop being dumb, mate. You do not have anything to apologize for. I made a state-ment, which sounded horrible if you did not know the back-ground. I would have been hurt too. You needed to know anyway. Jacob is…was…well still is, a big part of my life. He is buried at home. I still talk to him; he didn't have any family and if there is an afterlife where he can hear me, I didn't want him to be lonely. I can show you a portrait of him if you would like?" Emma asked hesitantly. She wanted her mate to know her best friend. They would have gotten along well, and she would like to think they would have become friends themselves.

"I would love to meet him. I envy you a bit, that you had such a great friend," he admitted softly.

"I would really like to share him with you. Rolf didn't really know Jacob. I never told him the whole story of Vlad's second attack, just that Jacob had saved me. Rolf missed Vlad by mere minutes, and I didn't want Rolf to blame himself for not getting home earlier. Jacob saved me from being violated again, Rolf saved me from dying. Samantha didn't join me until many years later, so I am the only one who still remembers and knows him. I'm sure it's a common occurrence when you live so long, but I try to keep his memory alive. I feel so guilty sometimes," Emma confessed in a whisper.

"He was a grown man who chose to defend his friend. He made his choice, and it was an honorable one. It shows just how great his character was. I think he would have wanted you to live your life, to be happy, not to feel any guilt over surviving. Just like you would want him to, if the situation had been reversed. I will be eternally grateful for him stepping in and saving you," Doc told her.

"Thank you, Albert. Thank you for understanding and for being willing to get to know each other over the phone. I don't know that I would have been able to get it all out in person yet."

"I love being able to talk to you. It does not matter if it is in person or on the phone. Although one day, I owe you a large hug for that story," Doc promised.

"Do you mind if we stop for the night?" Emma asked. She was exhausted now, but she did not want to insult her mate by dropping all that on him and then hanging up. "That really drained me."

"Go to sleep, dearest. Rest. I will see you Sunday for lunch." Doc tried to send calm and love through their bond.

Doc knocked on the Clan's front door. He was coming to pick Emma up for a date and wanted to start it off the correct way, well maybe the old-fashioned correct way. He knew he had a standing invitation to come in whenever he wanted, and even had his own key, but he wanted to treat Emma like she was special. He had a new bouquet of wildflowers in his hand. Doc had planned out an easy date, a picnic at the nearby park. It was supposed to be unseasonably warm today, and he thought a picnic would be a fun date. Doc felt uncharacteristically nervous; he would have thought that at his age he would be beyond feeling nerves. Maybe it had been the emotional conversation earlier in the week.

He heard the lock turn and stood up a little straighter, throwing his shoulders back. Doc sucked in a breath as Emma opened the door. She looked lovely, her hair in a loose braid down her back, the jeans hugging her curves, with a pretty cable-knit sweater. She was shorter than him, only coming up to his shoulders.

"Good afternoon," Emma greeted him quietly. "I'm looking forward to our date today."

"I'm glad; I have been looking forward to it as well. I thought we could go on a picnic today since it is so nice out. I have a basket packed with a few different things. I was thinking we could go to the park down the street."

"That sounds perfect!" Emma said. She watched as Albert picked up the basket he had sitting at his feet. She hadn't noticed it when she opened the door. After their conversation earlier in the week, they had kept the rest of their talks and texts on the lighter side. Being near him again, she felt the need to be closer to him. Feeling a little daring, she reached out and took his free hand. He glanced down at her in surprise and a big smile bloomed over his face. It was such a loving smile. She wanted to put more of those on his face, she decided.

The park was close, and it only took them a few minutes

to reach it, even with their slow stroll. Doc set the basket down to pull out an outdoor blanket. He smoothed it out and reached out a hand to help Emma down. Once she was settled, he started pulling out all kinds of foods: various vegetable sticks, apple slices, grapes, cheese and crackers, finger sandwiches with different fillings, bottled flat water and carbonated water, a few iced teas, and a thermos of hot tea. He had also packed small brownies and cookies for after lunch. He probably went a little overboard but had wanted to make sure he would have something she liked. He was still learning what her favorite foods were, although she wasn't a picky eater from what he had seen.

"This looks wonderful. Thank you, Albert," Emma said, picking up an apple.

Doc waited until she had eaten a few things before he took a bite. He wanted to make sure she got enough to eat; it was one of the quirks of being an old shifter, going back to days when food could be scarce.

Emma grazed, trying a little bit of everything. She noticed her mate ate a lot of the veggies and fruits. She wondered if it was tied to his animal, or if he just really liked eating healthier options. Emma was curious, but it felt rude to just outright ask him what his animal side was. Maybe a little teasing would get it out?

"Did you know that there may soon be bets about what your animal is? No one seems to know," Emma teased Albert.

She frowned when she noticed him tensing. That was not the reaction she had been going for. Her flirting and teasing skills must be even worse than she had thought. It *had* been over two hundred years since she had even attempted smiling flirtatiously at someone. "I was just teasing. No one is betting on your animal. It was just my horrible attempt at teasing you a little."

Doc sighed, forcing his muscles to relax again. "It's alright. I'm so used to hiding my other side that I haven't even decided when or how to tell the kids yet. Eventually they'll notice I never run with them or do other shifter bonding activities. It was never safe for me to do so before, but maybe with the protections around Rolf's house, it would be."

"Don't rush anything. If it is not safe, don't do it. They will love you regardless. I'm guessing you are one of the rare ones, if you've had to use that much caution," Emma replied, her last sentence a soft whisper.

Doc gave a miniscule nod.

"We won't talk about it here. When we're back on protected ground, you can tell me more, but only if you want to. You are still my mate, whether I know your animal or not."

"He wants to meet you. He is just very different and there are things you need to know before we would ever complete our mating," Doc warned Emma.

"You can tell me later," Emma emphasized once again. The park was empty, but she didn't want anyone overhearing something that could put him in danger. She may not be ready to complete their mating yet, but she felt a lot of affection toward the quiet doctor. She grabbed one of the finger sandwiches and plopped it in his mouth to keep him quiet.

Doc laughed behind the sandwich, but he dropped the subject.

6

Emma settled back into her bed, leaning against the headboard. It was almost time for her call to Albert. They never did get a chance to talk after their picnic. The kids had descended on them as soon as they walked in the door. It had been sweet that they were checking in on them and asking how the date went, but Emma still had been a little miffed that their conversation had been thwarted. She meant what she said though; even if she never knew what his animal was, Albert was still her mate. She would imagine it would be difficult to trust someone with a secret like that after so many years of hiding it. Not that she knew how old he was, but he was at least a little older than Rolfston and her.

Looking over at the painting on her dresser, she started talking quietly. "Jacob, I'm sorry I haven't checked in with you lately. It's lovely here; you would have enjoyed the hammocks. I love lying out there and reading. I'm getting better about going outside of the grounds, but it is still stressful. I wasn't this bad at home when I left, so I'm not sure why the anxiety came back again. New place, new people, seeing Vlad maybe. Although he's dead. I made it all the way to

Albert's one day and we had a lovely cup of tea. Of course, we ended up having the tea because I was almost to a panic attack. I've been to the bookstore as well and Albert bought me some books. We had a delightful picnic date the other day.

"I feel like we are the parents in this group sometimes. Not in a bad way, not that anyone here really needs a parent anymore, but more like we are older than they are, at least appearance-wise. I am not sure how old most of them are. Anyway…they all set off my motherly instincts. Rolfston is my child, Shaye my daughter-in-law, but I've sort of adopted the rest too." Emma laughed. "I think Albert has done the same, but he isn't as obvious about it. I think deep down he is still scared to have a group to call his own and does not want to push it. He can be such a silly man sometimes; the kids adore him. I've told him about you. Next time he is over, I am going to show him your portrait.

"I wanted to say thank you. I never would have met my mate without you. I wish you were here and could meet him. I think you would have been great friends," Emma added sadly.

She closed her eyes and could almost feel Jacob's hand ruffling her hair and a kiss on the top of her head. She swore some days she could sense him near her, but of course he wasn't there when she opened her eyes or turned to look. In all her time on earth, she hadn't heard many stories that were about real ghosts. Plus, she had never seen any evidence that Jacob was still earthbound. Not that she would have wanted that for her friend. She hoped wherever he was, he was in a happier place and had found himself a family. Emma shook her head at herself. Silly brain, she thought.

Emma grinned as her phone rang and she saw Albert's face show up on the caller ID. She had caught him at a moment when he had a big smile on his face and snapped a picture. It was fun being able to add a picture to the phone number of a person. It was the little things like that that kept amusing her through the years.

"Good evening, Albert. How was your day?" Emma asked as she accepted the call.

"It was surprisingly uneventful. I am hopeful the flu that has been going around has finally slowed down," Doc replied. It had been a good day at the office, just a few bumps and scrapes, nothing too major.

"Are you going to be able to join us for Thanksgiving?"

"Yes. I am closing the office that day but will work for a few hours in the morning. I want to catch up on some paperwork and make sure all prescription refills that are coming due are sent over to the pharmacy for the holiday weekend. You would be surprised by how many people wait until the last minute, even when it's a holiday and the office is closed. If I can be a little proactive and send them in to the pharmacy before a patient calls in a panic, it's a win. I should be over around lunchtime. It sounds like I should come hungry," Doc said with a smile. Tess and Shaye had both been bribing him with promises of food to attend Thanksgiving. It didn't take much convincing; he wanted to be there and spend time with his new family and mate. It would be the first holiday that he hadn't spent alone in a very long time.

"The kids may have gone overboard with the first official Clan holiday menu. Last I heard, there will be two different kinds of meat, potatoes, rolls, at least two types of pie. I am sure there will be a vegetable in there somewhere," Emma said with a laugh.

"I hope so. I would hate to have to lecture them on good eating habits," Doc agreed, smiling. He had heard rumors of said vegetables, but the last time he had spoken with Shaye about the holiday, they had not decided on what to have yet.

"How was your day?" Doc asked.

"It was good. I stopped by the farmers' market to get some things. I found a cute mini lemon meringue pie and had that for lunch. Well…I had two. They were so good though!" Emma exclaimed.

"Were they from the bakery? Mary makes the best lemon meringue I have ever had. It has just the right amount of meringue for me, not such a huge mound like at the grocery store," Doc replied.

"Yes! That's why I liked it too. I usually end up not eating half of the meringue topping, but this was a perfect amount," Emma agreed. "I really liked the market. Rolf told me that after Thanksgiving, it tends to be more of a craft market but there will still be a few food vendors. I was wondering if you would like to go with me one day to look for Christmas gifts?"

"I would love to. I haven't had to buy gifts in such a long time; I'm looking forward to it, but you may have to help me. I am not exactly up to date on what younger people might want."

"I'm sure they would like anything you gave them. We don't have picky kids; they simply love spending time with everyone. Plus, they are all adults, have good jobs, and can buy anything they need. It's simply about showing that you were thinking of them."

"We do have good kids," Doc agreed. "I never had any of my own, but I feel like I have adopted them. I know they are all capable adults; I think that it is that I am so much older than them and I tend to be more of a caregiver."

"Me too; although I'm not positive that I am older than all of them," Emma replied, laughing.

"I think you're older than most of them. I'm not entirely sure about Berkley." Doc smacked himself on the forehead. Don't say she is old, he scolded himself. "Not that you are old, you look beautiful. I am much, much older than any of you," he said hurriedly, trying to redeem himself.

Emma laughed at her mate. "I knew what you meant. I am completely aware that I was older when I was turned and have also been a vampire for around two hundred years. I'm older than most of the others in our group, both as a paranormal and as a combined age. I think I aged pretty well though. Probably from all the time I spent hiding from Vlad inside my house, less sun exposure."

"You are gorgeous, Emma. I am a lucky man to have such a beautiful mate, both inside and out." Doc loved how Emma looked. Her dark curly hair had a few strands of gray, her eyes had a few smile lines in the corners. She was a beautiful mature woman, who was also kind and loving. She had raised an equally kind and loving son and Doc considered himself touched by Fate to have met this group of amazing people.

"Thank you, Albert. I'm blessed to have such a handsome and understanding mate as well." Emma could feel her cheeks heating up and was grateful Albert couldn't see her blush. He really was a handsome man. His white hair made his dark eyes stand out, eyes that were always so kind. She felt like a young girl with a crush when she would catch herself looking at his picture on her phone.

Emma cleared her throat. "So. What size head do you have?" she asked, changing the subject.

Doc laughed. "What size head do I have?" he repeated, making sure he heard Emma right. "I'm not sure. Why?"

"I'm knitting hats for everyone. I'm not sure about gloves yet; I never really got the hang of gloves and I do not like wearing mittens. They don't give me as much control over gripping things. Maybe scarves or slippers to go with the hats? I'll figure something out. What are your favorite colors?"

"I like blue and green," Doc responded.

"Okay. I will measure your head at Thanksgiving unless I see you sooner."

"I didn't know you knitted. Have you been doing it long?" Doc asked.

"I learned when I was a child but really started doing it more after Vlad, when I was too afraid to venture far from the house. It gave me something to do. Later, Jacob would trade or sell them in town for things we needed. I used to make hats, scarves, shawls, and even a few sweaters or jackets for Samantha's children. I keep it relatively simple; I don't have the patience to do the extremely complicated designs. It keeps my hands busy and helps calm the anxiety. Plus, I love giving things to people I care about," Emma admitted.

"I tried crochet once," Doc replied, laughing. "I attempted to make a blanket, but it looked more like a net. The holes were way too big, so even if I used it as a fishing net, I could only catch something the size of a tuna or a small whale." It had been his first and last attempt at crocheting. He was not a very crafty or artistic person. He could heal people, bake a few items well, but things like drawing, knitting, or painting were out of his skill set. He could carve a few designs, mostly because he had years to figure it out and it was an easy thing to do when he traveled.

Emma laughed with him. She had a few creations that hadn't turned out well and been a waste of good yarn. Luckily, when she first started learning, she had her own sheep for wool. It made it a little easier and cheaper to learn. Emma grabbed out a pair of knitting needles and rummaged through her yarn bin. She was sure she had a blue and green that would go well together... Yes! she thought to herself when she found it. It was a nice soft yarn, perfect to make a blanket for Albert as a Christmas gift. Maybe a throw blanket, she mused. It would be great on his couch and perfect for when he decided to lie down for a quick nap. She knew he often took a power nap after work before dinner if he had time. Well, he called it a power nap, she called it falling asleep while waiting for dinner to cook.

"I've had a few pieces like that. It can be hard to learn a new pattern," Emma responded with a smile as she started on her new project. Maybe something with a wave pattern, something to make an inside joke out of Albert's attempt at a blanket.

"What other hobbies do you have?" Doc asked, interested. He was curious to all things Emma. He was also curious as to what hobbies or interests they might have in common.

"Hmm. You already know I love reading. I like feeding my loved ones and I am happy in the kitchen. I love gardening, so I was excited when Tess started talking about making a greenhouse. I came a little too late to get a fall garden planted, but I am planning a spring garden with Tess. I like animals; I used to sit outside and watch the farm animals. They all had their own personalities. It's a little corny, but I love watching the sunsets."

"We will have to take a walk down to the park or go take a drive through the National Park one night. Both are great for watching the sunset. The local park is probably better if we want to bring any snacks or a picnic though, less chance of bringing in non-shifter wildlife," Doc suggested. That could be a romantic date, maybe some candles, some wine. If it was a chilly night, there was a small community firepit that he could use.

"That would be fun. I would love that. We should do that before the snows come. I don't know that I'm adventurous enough to drive up and down a mountain in the snow."

"My SUV has four-wheel drive, but we can go before the snow gets heavy. We probably won't get too much before January, maybe a few inches," Doc replied. He had been maneuvering his way around the area for years in the snow, even back when it was rare to have a car and he took a horse instead. He had snow chains; although they usually didn't get enough snow to need them, he had used them before in other areas of the country.

"Do you decorate much for Christmas?" Emma asked. She

loved the lights at Christmas. It always made the winter seem a little bit cheerier.

"I put up a small tree in the clinic and a few lights outside. The town does a nice light-up of the main street, so I like to have at least something up. No one really comes to the house, so I don't have much on the inside."

"I can help you decorate, if you would like," Emma offered. She thought Albert could use some cheerful decorations in his space. He had been alone for too long.

"I would enjoy that. It would be nice to have it decorated if you came over for tea again."

"Then it's a date. We can go to the market for supplies and Christmas gifts and decorate your house." Emma was pleased. She was getting much better at making suggestions to her mate and she had planned an actual date herself. She was feeling more confident every day.

"Good morning, Tess." Emma laughed at the still sleepy-eyed girl as she came into the kitchen.

"Good morning. Thank you for getting the coffee started. I smell bacon too!"

Emma nodded. "It's in the oven. I also made up some breakfast casseroles that are baking right now. They should be ready soon. I thought it would give everyone something to munch on until dinnertime."

"Is Doc coming over for dinner?" Tess asked.

"Yes," Emma replied. She could feel her cheeks heating as a blush started. "He is going to work at the clinic for a few hours, just for calling in prescription refills and some paperwork. Emergencies are supposed to go to the hospital, since the clinic is officially closed for the day."

Tess nodded. "Where is Shaye? I thought she would have been down here already."

"I'm here. Just slow this morning. Oooo, coffee. Hello, my lovely," Shaye crooned at the coffee pot.

Emma shook her head. "I will never understand your love of coffee. Give me a nice tea any day."

"Just give it up, Mom," Rolf advised as he walked into the kitchen. "I have learned to never come between them and their coffee. Just hand them a mug and back away in the morning." He gave Emma a kiss on her cheek before grabbing a cup for himself.

"Luckily for you, Doc loves tea," Shaye teased over the top of her cup. Emma had to laugh at her daughter-in-law as she stood there breathing in the steam coming out of the cup, a look of joy on her face as she basked in the smell.

"He does. He has a lovely tea set as well," Emma replied with a tiny smirk.

The smell of bacon eventually drew out Sam, Ian, and Berkley, who joined them in the kitchen for the casseroles. Emma set aside a plate for Albert and one for Gawain, who was still in his room sucked up in his research. She was eager to see Albert today. She had a plan in place for their market date; she was thinking the week Tess and Sam were going to visit her family would make the perfect time to go shopping and decorate. It was the first full week in December, so the market would be switched over to Christmas and would leave plenty of time for Albert to enjoy the decorations they would put up. She just needed to check with him for a good day to go. She wasn't sure what his daily schedule would be like in the coming weeks.

The kitchen was full as everyone started making their dishes for dinner. The house was going to smell amazing in a little bit once everything was really cooking. Once the longer cook-time items were in the ovens, everyone headed out to the back patio to relax. The outdoor fireplace kept it nice and cozy, and she curled up on one of the couches. The boys all ran to the hammocks. Emma envisioned another hammock pavilion going in next year. This one had four spaces, but they needed more of them since the family grew. Rolf turned on the outdoor television so when the football games came on, people could listen or watch. Shaye and Tess were reading, so Emma ran inside to grab one of her books and a new cup of tea. It was so nice to sit back and relax with her family, she thought to herself, as she sank into the couch to enjoy her book.

Doc showed up around noon, happy to be near his new family. Emma gave Albert a quick hug, breathing in his comforting scent, as he came to sit by her.

"I left a surprise for you in the main fridge. It has your name on it," Doc whispered to her.

Emma studied his face. He had a slight grin, his eyes dancing with mischievousness and a good amount of fondness.

"What is it?" she whispered back.

Doc just shook his head gently. "It is a surprise for later. But it will be best today or tomorrow."

Emma tried to think of what it might be, before gasping. "Really? Did you bring me a lemon meringue?"

Doc didn't say anything, but his smile grew bigger. Emma was about to go inside to make sure it was safely hidden away. She had a small kitchen area in her room, though she rarely used it with the large kitchen downstairs. Her small refrigerator had the room to hide a pie. Unfortunately, she saw Rolf run inside, but he was back in a few minutes with Gawain in tow. He was carrying a fancy sheet of parchment paper and a pen, the formal document that would make them a Clan, a family, once they signed. Emma had not realized just how much she would miss having a family group near her. She should call Samantha and talk to her tonight, she thought to herself. Passing everyone a glass after the paper contained all of their signatures, Rolf raised his in a toast. "To our family. To the Nightwood Clan."

Emma took a sip of her champagne, but as soon as everyone started talking again, she ran inside to hide her prize. She slid back into her seat, Albert shaking his head laughing.

"Thank you," Emma said, daring to lean over and give him a kiss on the cheek.

7

Emma stood in front of her full-length mirror giving herself one last glance-over. Today was her date with Albert to the Christmas market. She knew she had no reason to be nervous, but she still felt a few jitters of nerves, her hand shaking a little as she finished the loose braid for her hair. She had on her favorite lavender sweater; she thought it made her blue eyes really stand out. Plus, it was soft and comfortable. She paired it with dark wash jeans, tight enough to show off her shape but not so tight that they looked like leggings, and a low-heeled boot. Emma twirled around, making sure she looked alright from all angles.

A knock startled her. Looking toward her door, she saw Shaye standing at the threshold.

"Mom, Doc is here. He is waiting downstairs," Shaye said with a smile. "You look really nice! That is a good color on you."

"Thank you. Is it dressy enough for what he is wearing?" Emma asked, suddenly concerned. She hadn't specified a dress code for the date and was hoping he wasn't too dressed up.

"I think it is perfect. He's in his corduroy pants and a

button-down shirt, nicer boots. He looks nice, but it leans to the more casual side. You'll have to let me know how the market is. I haven't been there yet. I'm still trying to think of ideas of what to get Rolf for Christmas. He seems to have everything already!"

"I'll keep my eyes open and let you know," Emma promised her daughter-in-law. She tried to swallow the rest of her nerves and moved to head out of her room.

Shaye grabbed her hand. "Doc really is a good guy, I promise. But," she emphasized, "if you get tired, stressed, anxious, unhappy, whatever it may be, just call us and we can come get you."

"Albert would never hurt me, not in any way," Emma protested.

"I know," Shaye added with a smile. "But the crowds might be overwhelming. I just want to remind you that you're not alone, and you have options." Shaye gave her a hug before walking downstairs with her.

Albert was waiting in the living room with a lovely bouquet of wildflowers. He looked very handsome. He was wearing his gray corduroy pants with a lovely emerald green shirt. His top couple of buttons were undone, giving her a slight glimpse of his chest. Not smooth, but not a bear either, just a smattering of hair. She felt the urge to grab hold and use the hairs to pull him toward her. Emma shook her head. She never felt these urges before. Her mate was pretty sexy though, she thought with a happy grin. His hair really shone against the darker color of the shirt.

"You look lovely, *agapi mou*," Albert complimented as he handed her the flowers.

"Thank you. You look very handsome. I like that color on you," Emma replied, with a slight blush. "Let me go put these in a vase, and I will be ready to go."

Emma hurried into the kitchen, smiling as she smelled the blooms. She loved that he remembered her favorite ones.

Bringing the vase of flowers back to the living room, she placed them on a table. Everyone could enjoy them while she was out; she would bring them up to her room when she got back home. She loved waking up in the morning and seeing the bright colors.

Albert held out her coat for her. "It's a little chilly out today, so I thought you might want your coat."

"Thank you," Emma said. She did get colder a little easier than some paranormals, it seemed.

As they headed out the door, she heard Rolf speak to her telepathically.

'Have fun on your date, Mom. Should I wait up?' Rolf teased, laughter in his voice.

'You shush. I am not ready for overnight visits yet,' she teased back.

'Ug. Nope, never mind. I do not want to know. Lalalala,' Rolf hummed back. Emma laughed, delighted that she still had the ability to gross out her son after all these years.

Albert looked down at her when a giggle escaped out loud. "Rolf was being silly," she said in explanation.

When Albert's fingers brushed against hers, she reached out and took hold of his hand. The smile she received in return was brilliant.

"Do you know what you are looking for? Or are you just browsing?"

"I don't have anything specific in mind, but I am looking forward to finding some unique things. I love the farmers' market and Rolf has sent me pictures of the Christmas market in the past; it always looked like such great fun," Emma replied, excited to explore with Albert by her side.

"I have walked through, but I don't think I ever really paid much attention to it before. I am excited to see what they have as well," Albert responded. In truth, he had wandered through in the past to feel like he was part of the community at the holiday season. He had never bought much, as he never had someone to buy things for. Well, he bought Sherri a gift every Christmas, as well as for her birthday and Administrative Professional's Day, but that was not the same thing. Now he had the opportunity to buy for several people. He was looking forward to finding something for Emma. She hadn't received enough gifts in her life from someone besides her son. He knew there used to be a someone at the market who made these wonderfully soft-looking scarves that she might like. But of course, maybe that was a silly idea since Emma knitted things as well. Or maybe she would like one that she had not made? Picking gifts for your partner was confusing. Maybe something would just jump out at him.

They walked hand in hand to the market. The Christmas Market committee had certainly transformed the open-air pergola-style market. The large structure looked magical. As Emma and Doc walked toward the front, they stopped to admire the newly decorated entrance that had been created with fir boughs woven together to form an arch. There were holly leaves peeking through the fir, with a sprinkle of white fairy lights. Emma looked up to find strings of snowflakes falling from the ceiling. The wooden beams were dotted with mistletoe and large ball ornaments. She leaned up and gave Albert a quick kiss to his cheek. She pointed up to the rafters when he looked down at her in surprise. He grinned and raised her hand to his mouth.

"Thank you, my dear," Albert said.

As they walked down the rows of booths, each aisle had been lined with lights, creating a welcoming atmosphere. Drawing in a deep breath, Emma smelled cloves and cinnamon. There was a low sound of Christmas music playing; enough to set the mood, but not so much that you couldn't hear the person next to you. It was such a festive mood; she was glad they had come.

"Did you and Rolf celebrate Christmas when he was a child?" Albert asked.

"Yes. My parents always tried to give me the best Christmas and I tried to do that with Rolf. Although, we're old enough that gift giving wasn't really a big deal like it is today. When he was a child, Christmas was more about the food. We started giving gifts and stockings after Rolf was an adult. I think we had both turned at that point. I wanted to keep with human traditions even though we were now vampires. After he moved to America, Rolf would make sure to come home for every Christmas. I can't wait until the kids start having babies; there are so many cute things available now!" Emma tried to contain her excitement. She knew babies were in the Clan's future, she just wasn't sure how far away it was.

"Looking forward to being a grandmother? You aren't that old," Doc teased his mate. In truth, he would like being a grandfather as well. Fate had granted him a lovely mate who already had a son and a found family that had welcomed him into their fold. He could see himself trying to spoil any little ones that came along.

"Yes! I had always wanted a few children, but after Vlad, I couldn't bring myself to be in an intimate position with a man again. Rolf was such a great baby. I'm sure they'll all make adorable kids. I'll enjoy being a grandma."

Doc held her hand as they continued to wander through the market. He knew he had to tell Emma about his beast soon. After she knew, he needed to tell the Clan. Doc hated keeping secrets from the people who were his family but knowing the secret could also put them at risk. His unique gifts were another thing they needed to discuss. There had been enough speculation spoken in dark corners among the few rare shifters like him, that there may be a gift he could share. His old mentor had also found a few documents to support the theory. The question was when or if to bring it up. It was a catch-twenty-two; it would help protect them, which would be good since they kept getting injured, but it would also paint a target on them if anyone found out.

He shook the thoughts out of his head for the moment. Now was the time to enjoy the market with his mate. Life-altering decisions could wait for another day.

"Would you like to share a snack with me?" Emma asked. She had been smelling the roasted candied nuts since they entered, and it was making her hungry.

"I would love to. What would you like?"

She pointed out the nut booth. "They smell so good!" she exclaimed. As they walked closer, her stomach grumbled.

Albert greeted the person and bought her a large bag and a hot cider. As they walked along, she spied a cute ornament booth. The woodcrafter had intricately carved tabletop-sized trees with tiny ornaments available to decorate with.

"I can make an ornament as well, if you don't see one here that you like," the man offered.

"Thank you, Tim. How are you? Are the kids coming in town for Christmas?" Doc asked as Emma started looking around.

"They are! Natalie just had a baby, so we're excited to meet our new granddaughter. Shelly is beside herself; she has a bunch of little girl clothes that she has bought. The boys are coming in too, but I'm not sure if they're bring anyone with them. So far, they haven't settled down. It will be good to see them, we weren't able to get together for Thanksgiving."

"Tell Natalie I would love to meet her daughter if she has time while she's in town! Congratulations," Doc told him. Natalie had been a patient of his when she was a child. He loved meeting his patients' children; it made him happy to see his patients thriving and happy.

He looked down at Emma. She had chosen a tree and was going through the little ornaments. The tree was beautiful, but he wasn't sure what she was trying to achieve. It seemed like she was looking for something specific in the plethora of ornaments, only picking a few here and there.

"What are you looking for?" he asked.

"I thought we could do a family tree and have an ornament for everyone. The coffee cup or book would be good for Shaye. Sam could have the wolf or beer mug. That type of thing," she responded.

"Hmm...here's a lovely little teacup for you," Doc said, handing it to her. It was a great idea and an easy one to expand on if the Clan grew.

They easily spent ten minutes looking over the different options. They finally found a unique ornament for almost everyone at home. Tim helped design a couple with them when they didn't find the right ones. Once the ornaments were made, Tim said he would drop them off at Albert's. Emma couldn't wait to see the tree decorated. She thought maybe when everyone was back in town, they could put the little tree out. She should get stockings for everyone and put their ornament in it for St. Nicholas's Day!

Doc laughed. His mate was certainly excited about something, she was bouncing. "What has you so excited?" he asked.

"I want to find stockings for everyone. I know Rolf doesn't put one up, but I think it is a cute tradition to start on St. Nicholas's Day. I can put their ornaments and a few treats in their stockings, and I could put out this tree and everyone could hang their ornament on it," she suggested. "Tess and Sam won't be here though, so should I wait?"

"That sounds like fun. I think they would be okay with waiting to open their stockings until they get home, or you can do it later for a Christmas Eve tradition if you want everyone to be there. May I help you stuff the stockings? I have the white hair for it."

"You do," Emma agreed. "But not the jolly belly," she added playfully as she poked him in the stomach. She could tell his abs were all muscle and no flab as soon as her hand touched him. She once again felt like petting him. It had been so long since she had felt attraction to anyone, but she didn't remember it being this strong. Emma allowed herself to lay her hand gently on his muscles before pulling away. "Should we see if there are any stockings?" she asked, blushing. She would buy the stockings and decide later if she would give them out for St. Nicholas's Day or at Christmas.

"Yes. I can't wait to see what else we can find," Doc replied. He was enjoying this date immensely. He was keeping an eye out for the scarf booth since he hadn't found anything else for Emma. There were a few small things, like the loose tea he had already placed an order for, and the teacup he thought she would love. His hope was that she would be over to his house more, so he had not bought Emma her own tea pot yet.

Suddenly, Albert pulled her to a quick stop. He was staring intently at something. Emma quickly looked around, trying to figure out what the problem was. "Albert? What is it? Is everything alright?"

"What? Oh, yes…everything is fine. I just saw the caramel apple stand and wanted to get one," he replied.

"A caramel apple?" she repeated back, a little incredulous that a treat could stop him mid-stride. Emma watched as a faint blush crept across Albert's face.

"Um…yes. A caramel apple. They're usually only available near Halloween, but I just saw the booth here and suddenly had a craving. Have you had one before? The best ones are with a tart apple, like a Granny Smith, and then the caramel coating, then a dark chocolate layer and a sprinkle of nuts. Sometimes things like chocolate chips are good too, but the nuts really give it a nice crunch and texture…" he trailed off.

Emma adored this side of her mate; she hadn't seen it before. He was so excited over something so small. And he was bashful about it! That blush was adorable. She grabbed his hand and started walking over to the booth. "Let's go get some. They should last several days in the refrigerator, so if we get a few you can have them for a snack later in the week," she suggested.

"Thank you," he replied quietly.

Emma had noticed before that Albert really enjoyed apples, so the amount of glee in his face as he looked over all the options should not have been such a surprise, but it was. As she thought about it, she wondered if it was his animal side coming out. There were some traits that different types of shifters seemed to have; predators seemed to like their burgers and steaks more on the rare side, strong smells were not pleasant to their noses and they avoided them, pack animals tended to enjoy larger friend and family groups, those with cold-blooded animal sides tended to live where it was warm, the reverse was true for those with cold weather animals. Albert was a bit of a mystery. He had been solitary, although he had grown up in a group. He didn't eat a lot of meat, so she didn't think he was a predator type. Well, he ate meat, just not as much as the carnivore types did. He liked his vegetables too, so maybe an animal side of an omnivore or herbivore. He lived in a lot of places, both cold and hot, so his animal part must be able to adapt to either. She was curious now, but she would never push him to tell her. Especially if it would put him in danger.

"What kind would you like?" he asked.

Emma hummed, looking over the choices. There was dark chocolate, milk chocolate, and white chocolate coatings. There were Christmas themed ones with red and green drizzles and sprinkles. White chocolate was a little too sweet for her, so she dismissed those. Maybe the dark chocolate with nuts, chocolate chips... Oh!

"I'll take the dark chocolate turtle, please," Emma requested. It looked delicious. The caramel coating was drizzled with dark chocolate, milk chocolate and covered in pecans and toffee pieces. "Can I also get a dark chocolate Everything?" This one had caramel, dark chocolate, pecans, toffee, chocolate chips, and pretzel pieces. She thought the girls would like that one. Tess and Sam had just left and wouldn't be back for a week, but she could set it out for dessert tonight and make sure it was as delicious as it looked. She could come back to the market next weekend to get another one. Maybe she would bring it to the clinic to share with Tess, Shaye, and Sherri. Emma had started to come over to the clinic for their Wednesday lunch break; it was their slow day and was also the day when Tess and Shaye had overlapping shifts. Tess did mostly paperwork and insurance claims for a couple hours on Wednesday afternoons. Although both the girls worked on Fridays, Emma had learned that was their busiest day and that no one seemed to have the same lunch break.

Doc placed his order for three different dark chocolate covered caramel apples: turtle, peanut, and pretzel topped. He paid for his and Emma's apples and took the bag from the salesperson, a little embarrassed by his earlier behavior. He couldn't believe his animal pulled him to a full stop like that. It's not like he didn't keep the beast supplied with apples all year long. For goodness sake, he even had a couple of apple trees growing behind the clinic. Granted, they didn't produce a lot of apples, but they still gave him some. Maybe he should ask Rolf if he could plant some at the Clan house; he just didn't have a lot of room in the small backyard of the clinic. Maybe then the darn beast would be satisfied.

Emma reached out and took his hand, so Doc was relieved that his earlier behavior hadn't made her keep her distance. What grown man goes gaga over apples? He made an effort to let go of his embarrassment and to simply enjoy spending time with Emma. He spied the scarf booth on the far side of the aisles. Every time they turned down an aisle parallel with it, he tried to crane his neck to see what was available. There was a gorgeous lavender one that he thought would look striking against Emma's dark hair. He saw Beth standing near the booth and quickly typed out a message one-handed as Emma looked through a stack of stockings.

DOC: Beth, would you be willing to buy that lavender scarf near your right hand? I want to get it for Emma, but she is here with me. I'll stop over on my lunch break tomorrow and pay you back.

BETH: Sure. Where are you?

Doc could see her looking around, so he did a quick wave. She smiled and waved back, before pointing to the scarf. Doc nodded, letting her know that was the one.

DOC: That's it! Is it soft?

BETH: Very soft. I'll have to tell Josh to buy me one of these scarves too, they're really nice. ;) You want a gift box for it?

DOC: Yes, please. Thank you so much! I didn't know how I was going to sneak buying that past her.

BETH: No problem! I'll see you tomorrow. If you see Josh, drop him a hint. Then I can act surprised on Christmas, lol.

DOC: I'll make sure he knows!

Doc smiled, happy he had a present for Emma. He pulled up Josh's contact information and sent him a quick message. He wasn't sure he would find the man in this crowd, but he wanted to be able to give him the idea for Beth. He turned back to Emma, finding her buying an armload of stockings. It looked like she was getting names embroidered on them as well. It was shaping up to be a nice Christmas. He could picture it already.

8

Doc could feel the pull in his lower back from being bent over his pile of books, but he wasn't moving. He was trying to scan them as fast as he could, scouring the text for anything that might help. At first, he had stayed where all his books were, but had moved to the living room to be closer to everyone, bringing a huge stack of the books he thought held the best hope. Doc could feel the tension both in the house and even in the family members that were not home yet. Emma was in the kitchen cooking up a storm; she was nervous baking. Everyone was on edge waiting for Tess and Sam to arrive. Doc had no idea what to expect when Sam got here. Tess told them about the attack on their way home and his injury, but Doc hadn't run into that type of magical interference before.

"Merri texted. They're almost here!" Shaye yelled, before running out the front door to wait at the gate. Doc looked up to see Berkley and Rolf run after her.

Shoot, he was hoping he would have had an answer by the time they arrived. Doc shook his head, trying to hurry through the last few books. When he heard car doors, he grabbed the books that contained mentions of an obscure healing practice that he only wanted to use as a last resort. The directions and repercussions were vague at best.

"Emma, they're here. I'm going to go out and see what the situation is," Doc yelled into the kitchen.

"Let me finish this. If you need me right away, call me and I'll come even with dough on my hands," Emma vowed. She had been in the middle of making bread. She didn't want to be in the way, as she didn't have a healing gift, but would do anything she could to help Sam.

Doc went running out of the house to the SUV. Placing the books on the floor of the car, he leaned in to check on Sam.

"How is he holding up?" Doc asked. Humming, he let his hands rest gently against the wound, his eyes closed, and head tilted in concentration. The witch who cast this spell was an evil person. He couldn't imagine killing someone for money. The spell was still trying to finish its job, but something was holding it back and he wasn't entirely sure it was simply because of the protection ward Tess had put up.

"Shaye, come here. I think if we do this together, we can get the spell out before we move him out of the car. I'm not entirely sure how the wards will react, so let's try this first. We will rely on the wards kicking the spell out of him as a last resort."

Shaye climbed into the back seat, placing her hands over Sam's side. Doc placed his hands over hers. "We are going to try healing first. If that doesn't work, we are going to try something else, like using magic to surgically cut it out."

"I didn't know you could do that?" Shay looked over at Doc questioningly.

"I have never tried it, but apparently it's something that can be done. At least according to my books. It's supposed to be extremely difficult to do, which may be why no one has done it in centuries. It is a back-up plan," Doc confessed. "Okay, focus on the spell itself, not the injuries. Let's see if we can't heal the spell, so to speak. Berkley, we may need you to give an extra push, so stay close." Doc really hoped it didn't come to that. He wasn't sure which was the riskier untried experiment: taking Sam through the gates with the spell still in him or trying a new type of spell removal.

Shaye closed her eyes to concentrate and was quiet for a few moments. "I can see it, almost like it's a living thing inside of him," Shaye said. Doc could see it as well, to him it looked like a vine trying to spread its poison through Sam's body. It was having a hard time reaching his heart to stop it, though.

"Tess, can you focus strongly on your bond for a second?" Shaye asked suddenly, excitement in her voice.

"What did you see?" Doc asked. He saw a reaction as well but wanted to compare what they were seeing. It may be able to help them save Sam.

"The mate bond is protecting his heart from the spell. When Tess focused, it glowed and pushed the spell back," Shaye replied. "Could it be that simple..." Shaye said, talking to herself as she looked at Sam through her healing gift. "It is a death spell and is clearly protected against witch magic. The mate bond is love, a special type of magic, right? It wasn't stopped by the spell. What about other love, like the Clan bond?"

Doc looked at her, surprised at her train of thought. "We do have a Clan bond of sorts. I wonder...it might work. If we could all join up, but not use any witch magic, only the Clan bond and the healing magic you have, we may be able to force it out. We would need everyone though and I'm not sure how to link everyone up. I think we would all have to be able to see it, to know where to focus the energy." It would be an amazing feat if it worked. Since they would be using the bond of friendship and family, he thought they would need all of them to be involved.

Doc watched as Shaye looked toward Rolf. Rolf nodded before telling them that he would try linking them all through his telepathy gift. Doc had forgotten that Rolf could use his telepathy with anyone; he was very respectful of personal boundaries. He watched as Rolf's face fell with disappointment when he couldn't connect to Berkley and Ian at the same time. Doc could see Rolf's muscles quiver with the amount of strain he was putting his body under trying to force a connection.

"I was able to reach Gawain, so it's not the distance. He had an idea, but everyone would have to be willing and it is a big ask." Rolf continued to explain that if they performed an old method of forming a Clan or Pack bond, they should all have a telepathic link to each other. The downside was that it was a forever type of bond, or at least extremely difficult to break, and included biting and a vow.

Berkley spoke up first. "We are family and Clan already. I don't see the problem with taking it further. I think you would make a great leader, Rolf. I will tell Ian to close the shop and head to the brewery to let Gawain know."

Everyone else nodded in agreement. Doc would do anything to help his new family, but he did hope that his animal wouldn't put up a fight with forming a bond to someone not his mate. He had no idea how he would react. Doc watched as Tess and Shaye worked to wake Sam up for a few minutes for the vow. It was quiet when Rolf bent over Sam, biting his neck. Everyone held their breath waiting to see what would happen.

"It worked!" Rolf exclaimed, moments later.

Merri ran inside to send Emma out.

Within minutes, the rest of the Clan was gathered and the process was repeated. Rolf looked a little overwhelmed once he finished and sat down heavily on the SUV's running step. Doc checked his pulse, finding it a little fast, but within normal limits. If Rolf now held the links for a telepathic bond to everyone in the Clan like the oath was supposed to forge, he could see where he would be overwhelmed.

"Okay. Let's try this again," Doc instructed. "Shaye, use your healing gift to show everyone where the spell is. Tess, you focus on the mate bond while the rest of us focus on the Clan bond. Send love, the sense of family and friendship, and any non-witch healing gift you have through the link."

Doc placed a hand on Sam as Shaye once again focused her attention on the wound. Seconds later, Doc felt a new presence in his mind, his animal glancing up and studying it, but was otherwise content. Huh. Who would have guessed? The beast seemed happy with being connected to everyone. Maybe he had been lonely as well. Shaye projected what she was seeing, pointing out the golden mate bond and the deep blue Clan bond. When everyone focused on Sam, the bonds shone so brightly they were almost blinding. Doc watched excitedly as the death spell retreated until it was a tiny speck. *'Everyone, try to send your energy through me like we did with Rolf. I'm going to target this last bit and see if that will work,'* Shaye instructed. The sheer amount of energy being let loose in the small space caused the hairs on Doc's arms to stand up. He watched through both his own healing gift and through Shaye's link as the spell burst and dissipated into nothingness. He could sense when Shaye sent out another quick search, making sure the spell was completely gone. Everyone gave a sigh of relief seeing Sam's wounds finally healing closed.

Tess grabbed Shaye into a one-armed hug, burying her face in her friend's neck and keeping the other hand buried in Sam's fur. Shaye hugged Tess tight. She really was turning into quite the healer, Doc thought to himself. He needed to find a way to train her better. He still had some of his old mentor's notes and goodness knew he had plenty of books that could help with her healing gift. As a vampire, she seemed to be better able to handle the strain it could put on her body, but some training couldn't hurt either.

Doc cleared his throat. "I think it is safe to move him

through the wards now. Let's drive him up to the front door and get him in bed. It looks like the saline bag is almost empty. I can get a blood transfusion and a new saline IV set up once we get up there. Gawain, you can head back if you need to. Ian, can you run to the clinic and grab me a couple bags of A+? Here is the clinic key."

Ian sped off, literally running. Doc quietly laughed. He didn't mean that Ian had to physically run, but with his speed it was probably quicker than finding a car and driving in. Gawain changed and flew back to the brewery. Rolf and Emma started walking back into the house. Tess climbed into the back seat with Shaye to keep an eye on Sam. Berkley climbed in to drive the SUV through the gates and Doc jumped into the front passenger seat. There was complete silence in the car as everyone held their breath as they drove through the gates. There was a huge exhale of air as they passed through without any problems.

Once they had pulled up to the front of the house, Doc and Shaye jumped out to get Sam's room ready. Doc went to a hall closet to grab the IV pole that he had left here after Rolf had been poisoned. If his kids kept getting injured, he may just have to commandeer a small room and set up a mini clinic in the house. He had kept some supplies here, but not enough if these types of events were going to keep happening. "I may need to start keeping everyone's blood type on hand at the house if this is going to continue," Doc grumbled. "If we don't need it, you guys can always drink it." With three vampires, he didn't have to worry about wasting the blood if it didn't get used.

"Stop being a grouch," Emma scolded gently as she came into the room and placed a kiss at his temple. "The kids are safe now." She knew Sam would recover, her previous visions had clearly shown him here in the future, so she allowed herself to not worry and to admire how sexy it was that Albert was worried about their kids.

With so many helping hands, Sam was set up quickly on the bed. Doc kept an IV kit out in case Sam shifted back to his human form and still needed one. Emma left to get food to bring upstairs for Tess; she was sure Tess would crash once the adrenaline wore off and wanted to make sure she had a full belly before that happened. Doc kept an eye on Sam as people trickled downstairs to grab their own food and brought it back to Sam and Tess's bedroom. Setting the plate near Tess, Emma turned to go back downstairs when she noticed Albert wasn't moving from the room. She filled a plate for them to share. He still seemed tense, even though they had healed Sam. Some food would help.

Doc stood in the corner trying to calm himself down. He tried to make sure his face didn't reflect any of his internal conflict. His beast was pacing in his mind, pushing him to protect their tribe. The beast had been present before and had been accepting of the other Clan members, but since they took part in the Clan blood bond ceremony, the animal seemed to have claimed them all as his own and took great offense that someone had threatened what was his.

'Calm down,' he told his beast. 'Shaye and I have this; Sam will be fine. What has gotten into you?'

The only thing he got in response was a push of *mine, mine, mine, my tribe, mine.* Doc sighed. He would worry about it later. He startled as he felt a hand on his face. His eyes looked down to focus on his mate, who was looking at him with an odd mix of concern and peace.

"Albert. I promise he will be fine. All my visions showed him in the future. You and Shaye have him on the road to recovery, so what is bothering you?" Emma asked.

Ah, the peace was the knowledge of the future and the concern had been for him. "People need to stop hurting our kids, or I may go gray for real," Doc tried to joke. "My animal is riled up for some reason. I was trying to calm him down, but he is still agitated," Doc admitted.

"Sit down with me and eat something. I'm sure you used some energy helping heal Sam. I made sure to grab you an apple. Maybe your animal just needs to sit and eat. Sometimes it takes a while to calm down after your adrenaline has been going. Being near you helps calm me, so maybe it will do the same for your animal side."

Doc took the plate from Emma, holding out a hand to help her sit down, before joining her. "Thank you for the food." His crazy beast did settle a little bit as he sat near his mate, but it was still wound up.

9

Emma took a deep breath as she left the house. She had volunteered to help Albert with some paperwork today. Shaye had offered to walk her down to the clinic, but she was determined to reach her mate on her own. Although she could drive a car, she wasn't comfortable with driving on the wrong side of the road yet and it was close enough to walk to. It was silly to have this anxiety about leaving the grounds still. She had eventually overcome it back in England, although usually someone from Samantha's family went with her if she went into town. Everyone here had their own jobs, even though she knew they would stop what they were doing to help her if she asked. It helped knowing that Tess and Merri were in town exploring, as well as Berkley and Ian, who were at their store.

She walked down the main street, focusing on her breathing. The smells from the bakery were almost enough to draw her in, until she saw the line. She would stop back when it was a little calmer. She passed the pottery shop, waving through the window at Ian and Berkley. They were helping a customer, but Ian came rushing out the door.

"Good morning, Emma! Where are you heading to?"

"I'm going down to Albert's. I told him I would help with the paperwork today."

Ian winced. "I heard he gets a wee testy on paperwork days. Would ye like me to walk wi' you?"

Emma smiled at him. He was such a sweet boy. "I need to do it on my own but thank you."

"Alright. We're both here if ye need anything," Ian promised.

She nodded and gave him a quick hug before continuing her journey. The bookstore wasn't open yet, but it looked like their window display had a few new books. Her anxiety spiked in social situations and dealing with crowds sent it soaring, so she tried to avoid the bookstore on the weekends. However, Albert provided a safe spot among the crowd, keeping her stress to a manageable level. Maybe she could ask him for another date to the bookstore. She finally reached the clinic and turned onto the sidewalk. Glancing down the street, she saw Ian had been watching over her. He waved before heading back into the store. Her son and daughter-in-law had made some great friends. Feeling proud of herself, she rang the bell on his personal front door. Seconds later, she heard feet coming down the stairs and the door opened.

"Good morning, *agapi mou*. Thank you for agreeing to help me today. I may have fallen a little behind with filing and created more of a mess for myself," Doc admitted sheepishly, kissing the palm of her hand. "How was your walk?"

Emma knew her Albert was also checking her pulse as he gave her a kiss, given the near panic attack she had last time she walked down on her own.

"It went well. Ian was worried, I think. He came out of the store and watched to make sure I made it the last few hundred feet to safety," Emma said, with just a smidge of self-deprecation to her voice.

"Your anxiety has been a part of your life for a long time, for a good reason, I might add. The job of a family is to help and support each other, so that is what he was trying to do without being overbearing, would be my guess. It will take time to settle it down and sometimes it may flare up again. Our goal is to have safeguards in place for when that happens. The Clan link will be useful, as well as having several of us working between home and the town. It's no different than the pendants Berkley made everyone to warn of danger. You are strong, you keep pushing yourself to go outside of the safety of your comfort zones. Now, stop being so hard on my wonderful mate," Doc scolded. He really did think she was strong to survive all that had happened to her and to keep trying to overcome her anxiety.

"Alright, dear. Show me these papers that need filing," Emma said to change the subject.

She followed Albert up the stairs to his office. She had not been to the dormered part of the house before. It had been renovated nicely into a large office. There was a small seating area with two comfortable-looking chairs, a small coffee table, and a half-bath. A computer and printer sat on a large table that was covered in papers and folders. The shorter walls of the house's dormer were lined with built-in filing cabinets. It was a great use of the shorter space.

"This is where I work after hours," he pointed out. "There are computers and a large capacity printer downstairs for use during clinic hours. I just hated having to keep running back downstairs for things when I was working up here. Paper files are normally stored here, but the laptops downstairs have the electronic versions to make it easier for Shaye and me. Sherri is great about inputting things into the electronic records, but she's been out of town visiting family and I was supposed to keep up."

Emma did surprisingly well with computers, probably from all the times she relied on it to order things for the farm or for herself, she thought. She had no problems filling in the electronic files if he ran her through the system.

"I can help input notes into the electronic records. Just walk me through your system and I'll get started," she offered.

"Thank you! I can work on putting the paper files away then," Doc replied, glad he had the help, but mostly happy to be spending time with her. He only hoped his darn animal settled down enough to fully enjoy it. It had still been pushier than normal, and he was starting to have a hard time controlling it.

It was pleasant sitting with her mate, helping him. It wasn't a hard task, just a little time-consuming. A couple of hours had passed when she stood to take a break and stretch. Emma looked down at her phone as it pinged. "Shaye said they are having a make-your-own-pizza night for dinner." Emma looked at Albert. "You're coming over for dinner tonight?"

"I haven't made my own pizza in years. It sounds fun."

"Good," Emma replied, glancing down as her phone pinged again. "Tess will be happy; she strongly hinted she wanted everyone at dinner."

"What's going on?"

"My guess is Merri either found or is going to find her mate today. She was very antsy this morning before they left."

Albert looked at Emma. Her eyes were twinkling in a way that made him think she knew more than she was saying. "You guess...or you know?" he asked in a teasing voice.

"Well, I know. Her mate is here, but she won't meet him until tonight," Emma confirmed.

"Hmmm...Tess wants everyone there for dinner and Merri hasn't met him yet...it's Gawain isn't it!" Doc exclaimed. It was the only thing that made sense, Merri had met everyone else at the house.

"Yes. I think they are a great match! I think she will make sure he eats, and he will make sure she has some adventures."

"They do seem like they will balance each other well.

That's a great reason to go over for dinner. I think we're almost done here, if you wanted to leave a little early and stop at the bookstore on the way home?" Doc asked.

"I would love that! They had some new books in the window when I went by earlier that I wanted to check out."

"Let's do that then. Let me finish this up, maybe about five minutes, and we can go browse, get a tea, and relax," he suggested.

Emma made sure to finish the file in front of her and saved it before stopping in the bathroom before they left. Albert held the door for her, following her out and locking up. She thought the decorations they put up looked nice. At least it looked a little homier and cheerier for when he was there.

She browsed through the bookstore, eager to find a new treasure. Albert stayed close by, looking at some other books as they wandered through the store. She had a short stack, three or four books that had caught her interest, when he leaned down.

"Would you like some tea? They have a nice jasmine blend that I tried last week."

"That sounds nice. Yes, let's get a cup and sit. I'm not sure which book I'm going to get this time. Ah! Just one book today," she said firmly when she noticed he was going to talk. "It will give me a reason to come back in." Not that she needed a reason to come to the bookstore.

"Alright," Doc conceded. He'd been going to buy all the books, but he would listen to her wishes. He might just make a note of the titles, just in case she didn't have them by Christmas. He could use them as stocking stuffers for her stocking, he thought with a grin.

It was quite nice sitting with his mate, listening to Christmas music. The time went quickly and soon enough Emma looked down at her watch, saying they had to go. Walking into the Clan house, Doc breathed deep, the scent of rising bread filling the air. Emma ran upstairs to put her book away. Doc followed to quickly check on Sam. He was pleased to see the wound was completely healed and everything seemed like it was back to normal. Doc took an unplanned detour into the library, thinking Rolf might have a book to help with his animal. Seeing Sam again, it had become unruly. It was like it had forgotten for a moment that Sam had been injured and once reminded had gone crazy. He flipped through a few books, but nothing seemed to have the answer he was looking for. If it kept up, he would go on the secret forum group for rare shifters. It was buried deep in the dark web; no one used their names, locations, or even their species, just in case hunters ever found the site. He had heard about it years ago, strangely enough from the Sheriff, so he could only guess that he was also a rare shifter. If Gage was on the site, then Doc felt a little better about its security. He went back downstairs when Tess called them to make their pizzas.

He thought Tess would lose her patience when Gawain did not come downstairs by the time all the pizzas were done baking. He exchanged an amused look with Emma when they noticed Tess's leg kept bouncing. Eventually though, Gawain came downstairs, and the new mates met each other. Merri was a little shy, but she warmed up quickly when they started talking about Gawain's research into a unicorn tribe. Doc almost swallowed his tongue when he heard that was what Gawain had been working on. Good grief, those were some long ago memories that were trying to come back to the surface. His animal side did not like those memories at all, conflicting with what it considered to be his real family.

After dessert, Doc said goodnight to Emma and quickly left to go home. He needed to change forms before his beast decided to come out on the street. Reaching his driveway, he rushed to the garage and locked himself in. He had the building redesigned when he added the addition to the house for the clinic. There were no windows, except for those high up and those were privacy glass. He made sure to grab some snacks out of the mini fridge and placed them on the tiny counter by the sink and filled the water bucket. As soon as the bucket touched the floor, his beast took over and exploded out of him. The change wasn't painful, but it was a shock to his system. It had been a long time since he'd shifted forms. Maybe the beast would finally let him know why it was so unsettled.

'What has gotten into you lately?' Doc asked, quite perturbed.

Mine.

'What's yours? Our new family? Yes, they are yours too. We need to figure out the best way to tell them about you and also keep them safe. You saw what happened to Sam; I don't want that to happen again and have it be because of us,' Doc tried to reason with his beast.

Mine. Mate. Tribe. Mine. Well, it certainly was stubborn and knew what it wanted.

'Yes, the Clan is our family now, and we are their family too. I still don't know why you are so upset.'

A hoof hit the floor in aggravation. His beast tried pushing feelings and thoughts at him, but as usual, it seemed muddled. Sometimes he really wished there were others like him to talk with to see if they had the same problem.

MINE. MATE. TRIBE. MINE. NOW. His beast practically shouted at him.

This was going nowhere. His beast didn't seem willing to give up forms again but was at least allowing Doc to control the body. This wasn't the first time he had to stay in the garage, and he had installed a sink with running water and a mini fridge when he renovated. He had some form of entertainment as well, as he had a large tablet installed on the wall. He had a wide-grip stylus that he had custom made that helped him navigate. It probably looked ridiculous as he had to hold it in his mouth, but it worked. It did take a long time to log in to the forum in this form since he had to type out everything one letter at a time.

Everyone was safe now, so he had no idea why his animal was so agitated. Doc spent hours exploring all kinds of rabbit holes trying to find something to help. His beast still did not want to relinquish forms. At least it couldn't open the garage door; he was pretty sure his beast would walk him right back to the Clan house. That would create quite the commotion in town.

Finally, about four o'clock in the morning, he found someone who had a vaguely similar situation. Before he dove into the thread, he sent an email to Sherri asking her to close the office and to reschedule his appointments for later in the week. When it was a more reasonable hour, he would send her a text as well. Shoot, he needed to send one to Shaye too since she was scheduled for today. Thank goodness his tablet was able to text; trying to text on his phone in this form was an exercise in futility. Hopefully his beast would back off and he could go into work tomorrow.

With his obligations covered for the moment, Doc started reading the thread he found. This person didn't seem like the same type of shifter, but also had problems connecting with his animal.

Anonymous3678: Like most of us here, I am an anomaly. I have never met another of my kind, so I am cautiously hopeful someone here can help. I met my mate, but they're human so I am taking it slow. The last thing I need is to trigger hunters to come to the area. I have managed to keep a quiet lifestyle in the city. I don't shift often, as I do not have a safe place, except for my apartment (which is really too small to do much but stand there once shifted). I have a few friends I have made here, a mix of human and paranormal. No one knows what I am, but they don't ask either. My mate got in a car wreck and was mildly injured (broken bone, but a clean break, easy to fix/heal). I was able to help heal them a little bit at the hospital, but since they don't know what I am, I simply sped the healing up, not completing it all the way. My animal is now driving me crazy. It won't stop yelling MATE at me and it is hard to maintain my human form. It just wants to claim its mate, but I don't feel we are ready for that yet. We never had the best relationship, the animal and me. I often feel separate from it, almost like there are two different entities in me. Any ideas to help? If I can't control it, I may have to leave, and I don't want to lose my mate. I think my animal would also fight for control to stop me from leaving, which if it was seen would cause massive problems.

Anonymous4852: Not sure how much help this is, but I feel the same way with my creature. I can sometimes talk to it, and it will use simple words or send feelings. Haven't met mate yet, so no help there. Just wanted to let you know, you're not alone.

Anonymous69: Just mate already. If you can't trust your own fated mate, we're all screwed. And not in the good way.

Anonymous25: No mate yet, but did find a new tribe/clan/pack/group/family. When I finally found people I trusted, beast came out more. Same separation feeling/problem. I don't get any words from mine, just feelings, which are not very helpful. I have telepathy and accidentally connected with a friend when they were injured and their own shields were down. Beast went nuts after that. Finally figured out it was trying to claim them as part of its tribe/clan/pack/group/family. The telepathy started it. Took forever to figure out what it wanted. Had to come out, so to speak, to friends to finish claiming them. Have to have honesty to form a true bond, so had to tell them what I was. Found a few references in some old books about forming own tribe/clan/pack/group/family with rare shifters. I'll attach images in case helps. Human side had started the claim by using telepathy, animal side then had to finish claim. Not much difference now except can connect to animal a little better, it's more content, I think. Can connect to all people in the claimed group now with telepathy, even those who weren't born with the gift themselves.

Anonymous638: *Not all of us have an animal that wants a group. Being alone is better.*

Anonymous950: *638, not everyone wants to be alone. Don't be a dick. Keep to the OP's problem or shut up.*

Anonymous876: *Look for Anonymous1.*

Anonymous638: *Don't tell me to shut up. I can say what I want.*

Doc skimmed the rest of the thread, but it looked like it devolved into arguing. Good grief, people could act like children. He wondered what the reference to Anonymous1 had to do with the original poster's problem. Before he started another search, he clicked on the attached images to see if they would be helpful. They were a little dark and blurry, it looked like someone took a picture with a cell phone. Oh lovely, he may have to translate part of it, Doc sighed as he read to himself.

When a unique shifter loses its tribe, the animal can feel lost. If the opportunity arises to form a new tribe, many times the animal will initiate a bond with trusted others. This is done primarily through a telepathic link… Shoot. Maybe that's what happened when Rolf created the Clan bond, Doc thought. *The animal side will become agitated, and quite adamant that these new people are theirs. Many a person has complained about an unrelenting whining of "mine."* Doc snorted. Yes, that was it. *To quiet your beast, you must complete the bond with your human half, as each part of you must claim them. However, be warned, everyone involved must be made aware and be willing to be claimed. You cannot simply claim random people to shut your beast up. Time and distance will cause the half-bond to fade, though it may take many years to completely be removed.*

Doc looked at the last picture. It was partially cut off. How in the world did one go about finishing the claim? he thought frantically as he scrolled to see if there were more pictures. Maybe the poster had another set of images? No. That was it. Great, now he didn't know much more than before. He started to reread the whole text again, hoping he would pick up on something he had missed earlier.

10

"Emma? Have you heard from Doc?" Shaye asked, concerned.

"Not since he left last night," Emma replied. Which was odd considering he almost always sent her a good morning text.

"I got a call from Sherri saying the office is closed today, that Doc wasn't feeling well. I have a text from him about six o'clock this morning saying the office was closed today and he'd 'hopefully see me tomorrow.' He didn't respond to my text when I tried checking in with him either, which he is normally good about."

"Let me try him," Emma replied as she pulled out her phone. She dialed Albert's cell phone first, but when that didn't get an answer, she tried the office phone.

"He's not answering either phone," Emma said. She was worried now. Albert had told her his type of shifter made him a target, and they had been talking about it at the park. What if someone had overheard them and gotten to him? "I'll go down to his office and check in. Maybe he forgot to charge his cell phone, and if he doesn't feel well, he probably isn't going to run over to the office side to answer that phone."

"Do you want me to go with you?" Shaye asked.

"No, you stay here. If I need you, I'll call," Emma said, tapping her head. She could use the telepathy from either the Clan link or her own gift to get in contact with them if she needed help. Something was telling her to go to Albert's on her own.

"Alright. Be safe and call if you or Doc need anything," Shaye replied. She still looked worried.

Emma grabbed her coat and Albert's house key. When he gave it to her last week, she had been petrified that he was asking her to move in with him already. Granted, in terms of paranormal fated mates, it had been a long time since they had met, but still short for her comfort level. Albert assured her that he knew she wasn't ready for more but wanted her to have access to his home. She was his mate and what he had was hers. It could be another safe place for her whenever she was in town.

As she got closer to the clinic, she could finally start to feel Albert along their bond. He felt disquieted, anxious. Something she was not used to feeling from him. It also had a wilder feel to it, not how he usually felt to her senses. Walking up to his front door, she noticed the porch light was still on. Did he not come home last night? No, she could sense him nearby.

"Albert?" Emma called out as she walked in the door. She searched the main floor but didn't see any trace of him. She hurried up the stairs, but he wasn't in the office either. There were no notes or papers lying out, so he hadn't been working late last night. Maybe he was over at the clinic? she thought as she opened the connecting door. Checking the clinic's office, breakroom, exam rooms, and even the reception area didn't provide any other clues to his whereabouts. Going back through the connecting door, she made sure to lock it on the house side. She could still sense him nearby, but where on earth could he be?

Emma went out through the back door, checking on the apple trees. It was rather late in the season for there to be any, but just in case… Nope, no Albert there either. She tried using their bond to locate him, but it was challenging since they hadn't completed their mating yet. There was only one other building on the property and that was the garage. His car was still parked in front, so he hadn't driven anywhere. Grasping the key, she went over to the side door. She paused when she heard scuffling sounds and a grunt. Emma hurriedly inserted the key and unlocked the door. If her mate was in trouble, she was going to help.

"Leave my mate a—" she started to shout as she entered. She came to an abrupt halt as she finally met Albert's animal side.

"Albert? Oh my," she whispered. "Is that you?"

At the head nod, she started moving closer, her hand held out in front of her, giving his beast time to scent her. "Can I touch you?" she asked in awe.

The large head lowered to nuzzle against her. A huff of air sounded next to her head as he lowered his head to lean against her shoulder.

"Love, no wonder you never tell anyone what you are. You are gorgeous," she praised him, as she glided her hands down his velvety nose, up around his ears. At a sound outside, his ears stood up and he shook his head with a whinny. "Let me make sure the door is locked." Emma hurried to lock the door before coming back to stand next to Albert's other form.

She stood still for a moment to really admire her mate. He was a creature of myth and legend. Even the other paranormals she knew had not seen one of his kind. His coat was bright white, almost glowing in its vibrancy. He stood tall, his head towering over her own frame; she would need a small ladder to climb on his back. His body was strong, the muscles in his legs looked like he could run for hours. She would love to see him running with his mane and tail flowing in the wind. He would look magnificent. Keeping one hand on him, Emma walked around Albert, learning this form. Reaching back around to his head, she rubbed around his ears and down his neck. Albert shifted, shaking out his wings. His feathers looked so soft to the touch.

"You want me to rub those too?" Emma asked. His wingspan was huge! Albert couldn't even open them all the way in the garage. His poor beast probably did not get out very much. She wondered if Berkely could adjust Albert's pendant to camouflage him while shifted so he could go out more often. Of course, that would mean he would have to tell the Clan about his animal, so she was probably getting ahead of herself.

Albert nodded his head again, so she lightly ran her hands over the feathers. They were as soft as they looked. Emma tried sending her feelings of affection and awe through their bond. It would be a little difficult to communicate if they could only rely on questions with a yes or no answer. She wondered if her telepathy would work with his animal side. Well, no time like the present to find out, she thought to herself.

"I want to try something. I'm going to try to talk telepathically and see if we can communicate that way. We won't get very far if we can only go with questions you answer with a head nod or shake," Emma explained.

'Can you hear me this way?' Emma asked, hopeful.

Albert nodded. *'Mine. Mate.'*

'I am your mate,' Emma reassured him. *'Why did you shift today? Did something happen? You never miss work.'*

'Clan mine. Mate mine. Clan hurt. Hurt MINE,' the beast stressed again.

'I am yours,' Emma restated. This wasn't like talking to Albert, it seemed his animal side was limited in speech, almost as if the human and animal weren't fully connected.

'The Clan is your family too. They will always be your friends and family, especially with the new Clan bond. Sam is healed, he's okay. The people who hurt him are dead.'

She got a frustrated huff of air in response. *'Mine. Hurt mine. Go mine. Mine safe.'*

Emma took a moment to think of what he was trying to say. She kept rubbing soothing patterns over his hide.

'We are all safe, I promise. The house has wards and protections on it. Everyone is now wearing their pendants that will alert them to danger. You want to go to the house? Is that what you mean by 'go'?' Emma asked, trying to understand.

She got a head nod in reply. *'Go.'*

'We can't go right now. It's too dangerous for you. Plus, no one knows about you yet. We need to come up with a plan to tell them that will keep you and them safe. There are plenty of people who would want to hurt you if they knew you existed, and they might try to hurt your family to get to you. I have an idea of how to help hide you so that you can come out more, but I need to check with Berkley first. Do you think that if I help you see everyone is safe through the Clan link, that you can let me talk to Albert? That way we can come up with a plan,' Emma tried explaining. She wasn't sure how much the animal side understood, if it was mostly instincts instead of logic.

Another head nod. Okay, this might work in bringing Albert back. She had a feeling that the beast was frustrated and trying to keep control of the form. She closed her eyes to concentrate, keeping a hand on his neck. First focusing on her mate bond, she felt the beast's need to know its family was safe. Emma then gently reached out along the Clan link, not trying to talk to or disturb anyone, just enough to feel that they were healthy and safe. It was easiest if she concentrated on Rolf first, as she had a lot more experience using telepathy with her son, before slowly traveling along the link to check in with other Clan members.

'See? Everyone is safe,' Emma said. *'I loved meeting you. May*

I speak to Albert now? I will help him find a way to introduce you to the Clan and then maybe we can find a way you can run at the house.' She pressed a kiss to the velvet muzzle, careful to avoid hitting her head on the horn.

He took a step back, the air shifting around him until Albert the human stood in the animal's place.

"Thank you, dear. He has been a stubborn twit since yesterday. It was brilliant showing him that everyone really was okay. I'll try to let him connect with them that way more."

"An alicorn, Albert?" she questioned incredulously. She had seen his animal form, the horse body with wings and a horn of all things. She knew what he was, but she had thought they were all myths.

"Let me grab the tablet, I was trying to do some research while I was stuck, and then we can go to the house for tea. I could use a snack too. Are you hungry? I can make us some food. Would you like brunch or lunch, or just a munchy type of snack?" Doc kept rambling. He was a little scared that Emma would decide his animal half was too much to deal with. After all, his own tribe had kicked him out the second he was considered an adult. He knew he didn't have many trusted friends and he feared losing the ones he had. Funny how quickly he had become attached to them after so many years of being alone.

Emma followed him inside. She wasn't sure what to say to reassure him. She could feel his nervousness through their bond. Once the door was closed, she grabbed his hand before he could distract himself with the tea kettle. "Albert, whatever is going through your head is probably not right. Why are you so nervous?"

Doc sighed. "Let me get the tea going, and we can sit and talk on the couch. I'm ready to sit after standing all night. I'll try to explain then, if that's okay?" He tried to gather his thoughts in a reasonable order as he went through the normally calming process of making the tea. He picked the jade tea pot, hoping that the properties of the jade would help them today.

As they sat, Doc handed Emma her cup first. "I'm worried about sharing my animal with everyone. As ridiculous as it sounds, some part of me is worried that it is just too much to deal with and I'll be asked to leave like I was with my birth tribe. I've been alone a very long time and it has been nice having a family group again."

Emma laid her hand on his leg. "You are being ridiculous," she agreed. "We're mates, that is a forever thing. Fate doesn't make mistakes, and I believe all of us meeting and forming a Clan, our own chosen family, is part of Fate's plan. Now, tell me the whole story. You've told me a little bit but start at the beginning and tell me all of it this time," Emma ordered gently. She had a feeling that it was a little worse than he had let on previously.

Doc sighed. "My heritage is Greek, but we were on this land long before Leif came over. I'm not sure how long we were here, but I do know that I was born by the time Leif visited. We wanted to find wide open spaces to run without people hunting us. The same stupid reasons exist today; our horns do not have magical powers to keep you from being poisoned. A lot of us had some level of healing gifts though, so the rumors persisted. Strangely, Gawain is almost on the right track to find the remains of the unicorn tribe. At least, one of their locations. We moved around a lot when I was younger, before we finally settled for several years in one spot. Unicorns do not shift until around puberty, probably to make sure we don't accidently shift near humans or hunters. Once there were several of us nearing shifting age, the tribe settled in one spot so that we could learn how to shift, to contain ourselves. It's hard to focus on learning to control your urges when you are constantly on the move." Doc paused.

"Your whole tribe was made of unicorns?" Emma asked, trying to clarify.

"Yes, sorry. Everyone was a unicorn, although just like horses, everyone's coat varied in color. Even horn length can vary. I told you about how my parents were hands-off; I don't think they even really liked each other. The tribe leader arranged their mating, hoping to produce a strong generation. As far as I know, he arranged all the matings in our tribe; I'm not sure if any of them were fated mates, but my parents most certainly were not. I was born here in this land, not back home in Greece. I was an only child. I had lots of friends near my age. Even the older children would play with the younger kids because there just wasn't anyone else to interact with. I often hung around the older kids because my parents did not pay much attention to me, other than ensuring that I left with the tribe when it was move day. We were a very insularly group, not encouraged to socialize outside of our tribe. Occasionally we would come across people to trade with, but when we did, it was strictly business. It wasn't a bad life though.

"Puberty is what changed it all. I shifted and suddenly I was different from anyone else in my herd. I had the horn of a unicorn, but the wings of a pegasus. There had never been an alicorn in my tribe and the leader was not pleased, to say the least. He was probably worried about drawing even more attention to us and having increased danger because of me. He couldn't kick me out because I was still a minor under our laws, but he could make it very uncomfortable for me to stay. He basically encouraged everyone in the tribe to shun me."

Emma watched as Doc unconsciously rubbed at his chest. She could feel the pain of the memory through their bond.

"I got lucky though and one of the elders took me under her wing. I stayed at her house more often than my parents'. Their level of care decreased even less, to the point that there was no food kept in the house. Thalia would feed me and help make me new clothes when my others became too tattered or small. She taught me how to sew enough to fix my clothing and how to forage and make my own food. She was the one who encouraged me to fly, patching up my scrapes when I fell. Thalia was also the tribe healer and she taught me the craft. When the tribe moved to this country, she brought a few books and papers with her from home and her previous travels. There were a few references to alicorns. Any time she had a chance to interact with someone outside of our tribe, she tried to find more information about my animal for me. Eventually the time came that I reached adulthood and was forced to leave."

Doc took a shuddering breath. He didn't want to go into detail about that day, it was burned into his memory. The last visual he had of most of his tribe was lying on the ground, bleeding from the beating the tribe leader, his old childhood friends, and even his parents had given him. Thalia had heard the commotion and stopped them before they could kill him. Shielding his fallen body with her own, she had forced them to stop because harming an elder was punishable by exile or death, depending on the injury. She had dragged his body to her home, patching him up. She packed him a bag full of the manuscripts she had collected, written down the rumors and legends she had heard as a child, and given him some food and supplies. She had packed what dried meat and vegetables she had, along with half of her healing supplies. Thalia had collected or traded her services for trinkets occasionally over the years, and she gave him those to trade for things he might need along his journey. He remembered her wrinkled face looking up at him, love in her eyes, as her gnarled hands held his face. 'Listen to me, *yiós*. You are special, no matter that these people are too dimwitted to understand that. Learn more healing, use your skills to live your life. Protect your identity; these are not the only ignorant people out there. You will find a family that deserves you, it may just take time. Do not be afraid to love them. If the legends are right, you will have that family forever if you take the chance. Now, take this and go. If you want to come visit, there is a large tree on the outskirts of the village. I can see it from the back of my house. Tie a ribbon or something to a branch facing this window and I will meet you there the next day. Be careful coming here, these people will not be kind. If I find anything else about your beast, I will save it and give it to you. I love you like you are my own son. Now go and take this for your mate. She will be perfect for you, brought to you when Fate knows you are ready.' Thalia had handed him a bracelet, the one she had received from her own mother, brought with her from the old country. She had never taken it off before. It even was charmed to stay with her during a shift. Doc had tears in his eyes as he left her behind; she had called him son and in truth, she had been more of a mother to him than his ever had.

Doc cleared his throat. "Anyway, it was not a happy send-off. Thalia was the only one still left in the tribe that cared for me. She sent me off with a bag of supplies. I went back several times over the years, sneaking around the back and meeting her at our tree. I would bring back new techniques or herbs I had found for healing, sometimes trinkets that I thought she might like. When she had new information about my beast, she would hand me the information she had found. Eventually old age took her away and she was no longer waiting for me at the tree. It was a long time before I passed by the tribe again. They were all gone when I finally returned. I found markers for my parents. It did not look like the village had been attacked, more like it had fallen in disrepair from age and neglect. I don't know if insularism, a lack of new members and old age took them all, or if there were survivors and they had moved on. I travelled, using my healing skills to support myself. I went to medical school as well, repeating it every forty years or so to keep up with new trends. Eventually I settled here in Rockfort. I enjoy the people in the town but haven't had many close friends since I keep my shifter side a secret."

Emma held his hand, staying quiet for a moment to digest everything. If he was here before Leif Erikson came to America, then he was one of the oldest shifters she knew. "Albert, how old are you?"

"A little over two thousand years old, give or take a few years. I've lost track. I know I was born in the winter, which was not common. I'm not sure what day or month. We didn't really celebrate birthdays."

"We'll have to pick a day for your birthday then. I bet you have missed out on many birthday celebrations and that needs to change," Emma stated firmly, pressing a kiss to the back of his hand.

"Maybe in January? That way it doesn't interfere with Christmas."

"It can be whenever you want. You get to pick."

"Let's do January sixteenth," Doc replied with a small smile.

"Did you always have white hair? Since I'm younger than you, do you think your lifespan will lengthen to match the time I have left? I'm not sure how that works," Emma asked, concerned. Her mate was much older than she was, and she wanted to have as much time with him as possible.

"Oh…um…well, see…" Doc stumbled over his words. He wasn't sure how to get this part out. "This was part of the things we had to finish talking about before we complete our mating. My hair turned white when I shifted for the first time; it was a dark brown or black before. I'm still not sure what made it change.

"I don't interact the same way most shifters do with their animal sides. It's almost like we are two separate entities in the same body. I am on a secret forum that has other rare shifters, and it seems like a common problem for us strange ones. I have not been able to figure out why yet.

"So, in addition to that oddity, we have a longer lifespan than the rest of the shifters. The rare ones, I mean. I stopped aging around forty or so. I haven't changed since then. The rest of my tribe has passed, as far as I know. It seems like because there are so few of us, that we live really long."

"How long, Albert?" Emma asked. She could feel his nerves and reluctance to answer along their bond. What was so bad that he was afraid to tell her?

"Forever?" Doc answered.

Emma sat back, staring at him. Was he being serious? How could they live forever? "What?"

"As far as I can tell, the rarer your paranormal species, the longer lived you are. Witches are pretty darn commonplace and they only live to around two hundred, vampires and most shifters to about two thousand if they are lucky, bird shifters are a little more common and they live to about one thousand years old. The Fae are smaller in numbers but are the only somewhat common species that I know of that are immortal. I'm not sure about the dragons yet. Unicorns live to about three to four thousand years. I've been piecing together information using what Thalia found for me and my own findings. The forum I am part of seems to support the research I've done. It seems like there are less than a handful of the oddest of us. We tend not to disclose our species, in the event that if hunters were to hack the site, they couldn't track us down. I've met a medusa, a selkie, a sabretooth, and a few others on my journeys. Alicorns seem to be one of the rarest; I haven't met another one like me yet."

"Both your parents and lineage were unicorns?" Emma asked, trying hard to understand.

"As far as I know. There was a hushed rumor that there was a pegasus mated in long ago, but I never found proof. I wonder if it's a genetic mutation since it seems like the rare shifter has at least some common base to their parents. Take me for example: I turned out to be an alicorn, my parents were unicorns, but both are horse based. I mean, there is the case of the centaurs which started out as a genetic anomaly as a shifting disorder where they could not shift fully into their horse. Because of being ostracized, they tended to mate with each other, thus cementing the genetic code for generations to come. Or maybe Fate likes to keep it interesting, I don't know. But from what I've found out, I'm one of the immortal ones. If you accept being my mate, you would be immortal too."

"I would bury my son and almost everyone else in the Clan, except for Berkley and Ian, assuming Ian received Berkley's immortality when they mated," Emma stated. She was trying to stay calm, but how could Fate give her a mate and then expect her to watch her son die before her. Emma could feel her breathing start to speed up, on the edge of a panic attack. Her stomach started roiling.

"Emmaline. Look at me," Doc commanded in a firm voice. This was not going as well as he could have hoped. Once her eyes were on his, he sent calming vibes through their bond.

"It doesn't necessarily mean that. We can simply keep dating and not complete our mating. There may be another option, one I have been trying to verify. I was working on some research last night when I was stuck in the garage," he tried to explain.

"What's the other option? I do want to be your mate, but to outlive them all is just..." Emma trailed off, tears in her voice.

Doc felt his beast rear up. *Mine.*

'I know she's ours. But no one wants to outlive their family,' Doc tried to explain.

Mate, mine. Clan, mine. Mine, always. Mine, no go, his beast replied adamantly.

Doc had the feeling it was trying to tell him something.

'Forever? They would live forever? They could be immortal too?' Doc asked his beast.

He got the sensation of a head nod and satisfaction. Huh. Maybe his research was right after all.

"There are stories that hint that I can share my immortality with people besides my mate. I think it was meant to keep the tribe together, maybe as a safety net for the alicorn or another rare shifter if they can share it as well. I'm still trying to find the answer as to how. When Rolf initiated the Clan bond, it woke something in my beast. He kept claiming 'mine' and wouldn't shut up. When I got back here, he took control and shifted. I have a tablet and thicker stylus I keep in the garage for the times when I am in my animal form. I was on the forum trying to find an answer to why he was being so unreasonable. It seems like it happens when the beast is ready to make a new tribe, or whatever your species calls it. The animal and human side both need to claim the other person or people, starting with a telepathic link."

"Did your beast take the Clan link to mean the claiming had started?"

"Yes, and since I was human at the time, he wants to claim everyone too. That will finish the claiming, in that he views it as his tribe, but I have no idea yet if that will also transfer the immortality or if that is a different action altogether. I do know that the other party must be aware and consent or the bond won't form. I haven't finished looking through the forum yet," Doc finished, taking a sip of his now cold tea.

"I can help you look. It would be wonderful if we could all be together, and we don't have to watch our kids go before us. Plus, it would be helpful since they keep seeming to be attacked. Why don't you show me this forum and what to look for and you can lie down to nap while I read?"

The beast took over for a moment. *'Mine?,'* he asked Emma.

'Yes, I'm yours. I am sure the others would love to be part of

your tribe since you are already part of the Clan. But Albert is right, and we need to first tell everyone what type of shifter you are. They need to know before they can accept the claim.'

'Mine safe?'

'They're all safe. Do you want me to show you again?' Emma asked.

Feeling a gentle nudge in response, she opened the Clan link to the beast, allowing him to see they were all safe and healthy.

'Mine,' he replied, contentment in his voice.

"Albert, you might need to let your beast connect over the Clan link more often, just so it feels reassured that everyone is okay," Emma advised. "Now, lie down and I'll start reading if you show me where you left off," she told him, patting her lap.

Doc grabbed the tablet and a pillow, placing it in her lap before lying down and showing her the forum. "This is where I stopped. One person said to look for Anonymous1. I don't know why, but that was going to be my next search."

"Alright. You get a cat nap in, and I'll wake you if I find anything."

Emma started reading, enjoying this time with Albert. He was asleep within a minute of lying down. As she started reading in the forum, she could see how he had been sucked in last night. Some of the posts were very informative, if not a little dry. Others were like looking at a train wreck, you wanted to look away from the drama, but something just kept pulling you back in. As the minutes turned into an hour, she felt like she was looking for a needle in a haystack, nothing from Anonymous1 so far. Hmm, she thought, maybe Anonymous1 was the creator of the forum? She finally decided to start at the introduction post and see if she could find them. Yes! she thought to herself. Anonymous1 was the very first poster. Emma started skimming, looking for something that would jump out at her.

Anonymous1*: Welcome to the only forum dedicated to extraordinary, rare, weird, strange, 'am I the only one' type of shifters. I myself am a strange sort of shifter. I am the oldest of any shifter I have met by thousands of years. One of my gifts is to be able to sense what type of shifter someone is, no matter if I haven't met one of their kind before. I realized that most of us were different animals than our parents or others in our tribe/Clan/Pack/family group. I spent years digging through old legends and documents trying to find information that would explain what I am. I wanted to share this with you. I have this forum buried pretty deep and have several magical and technological securities around it. Please make sure you only log in after following the following protocols…*Emma skipped ahead. She wasn't super tech savvy and Doc seemed to have already followed the instructions. There was an updated note at the bottom of Anonymous1's post that was dated a few months ago. *I have several files on this forum with the information I found. We seem to be even stranger shifters, in that we may be immortal. We can have mates, like any other shifter, and can share our immortality with them. Now, your beast may get restless after a while and will try to claim a group as their own. Be careful who you claim as your tribe/family/Clan/Pack, you may inadvertently claim them forever. See Claiming folder. They have to be willing to be claimed and both you and your beast must be in agreement. You may be able to share your immortality with them after forging the claiming bond. New folders include: Mates, Claiming (including a brief course in how to keep your thoughts to yourself after you all have a telepathic bond), Hunters, Types. Do NOT type what genre or type of shifter you are. This is just a list of ones I have come across. Never give out identifying information, including your species, in the unlikely case that hunters would be able to hack into this forum.*

Emma cheered and lightly tapped Albert awake. "I found it! Albert, wake up! I found him!"

Doc slowly blinked his eyes open. "You found him?" he asked, trying to focus.

"I did. I think Anonymous1 started the forum. There are all kinds of documents that he has uploaded. He briefly mentioned claiming a tribe and sharing immortality. There is a folder that is supposed to have the documentation he found on it. Here, start reading and I'll make new tea," she instructed as she handed him the tablet. Once he sat up, she ran to the kitchen to get the kettle started. This could solve everything.

11

Emma was hiding in the kitchen under the guise of checking on the food. She was nervous to have the Sheriff come to their home. He had helped them with the a-hole Vlad and was a Warden, so she knew he was probably a good man. He was just so huge though! He was taller than her son and Albert. Tess had warned her to expect his magic to be overwhelming. She had wanted Emma to be prepared ahead of time and not frightened when the man showed up.

"Em, it will be fine. I promise you. He is a little overwhelming, a little intimidating, but I would never allow him near you if he was a threat," she heard Albert say as he came up behind her. She was getting better about not jumping every time she was startled. It helped that Albert tried to make a noise or announce himself before coming too close to her. "I have known him, at least in passing, for a long time and I have never gotten a hint of malice from him. Plus, the wards won't let him in if he isn't a good person," he reminded her, his voice soft and calm.

"I know. I'm just nervous," Emma replied as she turned around from the stove.

"Can I give you a hug?" Doc asked. As she nodded, he

wrapped her in a loose hug. They had come a long way since the first day they had met. He had told her the truth; he would never allow someone to harm her again.

Emma allowed the warmth of his body to relax her nerves as she leaned her head against his chest and breathed in Albert's scent. Her family would protect her, she knew that. It was just that the anxiety sometimes got the better of her. After a couple of minutes, she stepped back.

"We better go help set up," she said, giving Doc's hand a quick squeeze.

Stepping out onto the back porch, it looked like they had already made good use of the time and moved some tables and chairs around. The fire was blazing and the hammocks were hung.

"Are we hammocking during dinner?" Emma teased. She knew the boys used any excuse to set up the hammocks.

"No, but if we have time before or after dinner, we might as well make use of the dome keeping in the heat from the fire." Sam grinned.

Emma just had to smile and shake her head. If Tess wasn't around, she was sure that Sam would find a way to live in a hammock.

"The soups are ready. I was thinking of having the food set up out here, maybe place a table near the grill with plates and bowls, the steaks when they are done grilling, the salad, the soups, and the rolls. Make an assembly line?" Emma suggested.

"Sounds like a good plan, Mom," Rolf replied.

It only took a few minutes to get it all set up with everyone helping.

Tess looked toward the front of the house. "Someone just came through the gates. It's probably the Sheriff. I'll go walk him around the back," Tess offered before going into the house. Sam started to follow her.

"Rolf, I'll go in with Tess and let Gawain and Merri know it's time for dinner," Sam said.

Moments later, Emma heard voices approaching from the side of the house and moved closer to Albert. Watching the corner, she saw Gage walk in with Tess. She could tell the Sheriff was old, just a vibe she got from him. She watched as he approached Rolf first, typical of an old-style greeting to a Pack or Clan leader.

"Thank you for the dinner offer. It's nice not to eat out in town or try to make a meal just for myself," the Sheriff said, holding his hand out to shake Rolf's.

"I think you know everyone here, at least by sight, but I will make introductions just in case." Rolf went to stand by each of his Clan members as he introduced them. "This is Shaye, my mate, Tess and Sam, Berkley and Ian, my mother Emmaline and Doc, Gawain and Merri, our newest member. We welcome you to the Nightwood Clan," Rolf stated, his tone strong and formal.

"Greetings. It is an honor to meet you all. Thank you for the dinner invitation," Gage told them, inclining his head in greeting at the end of the introductions.

Tess glanced at Shaye and they both rolled their eyes before giggling.

"Girls," Emma said softly. She laughed quietly, knowing the girls were trying to lighten the mood. It was a rather stuffy start to the evening, much more formal feeling than their usual dinners.

Tess and Shaye started laughing again. "Sorry, Mom," they said in unison.

"They are being ridiculous," Tess complained.

"Our kids have a point," Doc joined in. Emma loved that his eyes were sparkling. He was having fun.

"See! Doc Dad knows what we are talking about." Tess grinned, clearly pleased with the nickname she created for Albert.

"I'm not sure about the name Doc Dad," Doc voiced his complaint with a smile. He loved being able to join in the teasing though, it made him feel like part of the family.

"It does have nice alliteration," Merri quietly inserted.

Rolf sighed, looking around his family. Emma knew that he had wanted to make a good impression, but being themselves, the warm, welcoming family they were, would make the best impression. "Welcome to our house, Gage. We are loud, a little crazy, but we are a family. We don't really have a formal structure like many Packs or Clans do, it's really on paper only. I guess what I am trying to say is, welcome. Feel free to be yourself," Rolf added.

Sam laughed. "We are easier to handle on a full stomach and a beer. Would you like one?"

"I would love to try the new Christmas one, if you have it here. I have heard good things through the gossip mill. I normally eat at the brewery on my lunch break, but I don't drink since I am on duty."

"I did bring some home. We've been selling a lot of it, so I think it will come back next year," Sam replied happily. He went to the cooler to get a bottle for the Sheriff.

"Steaks are ready!" Ian shouted from the grill.

"We are doing buffet style, so feel free to grab whatever you want. There is steak, baked potatoes, salad, rolls, a tomato-basil soup, and a tortilla chicken soup. We always seem to make too much, so eat as much as you want," Shaye told Gage. "There will be ice cream cookie sandwiches for dessert. Mom made some sugar cookies this afternoon and they are delicious!"

"I knew there were some missing!" Emma exclaimed, glaring at her formerly favorite daughter-in-law. She had thought she had made enough for three dozen sandwiches, but she had ended up with closer to two dozen. The boys loved to eat, so she always tried to keep snacks on hand and had planned on having leftovers for the freezer. At least she knew she wasn't going crazy, she had made enough cookies.

"I only took one!" Shaye protested.

Emma simply shook her head at her. She had seen a few others sneaking in and out of the kitchen when they thought she wasn't looking. Shaye probably did only have one, but Emma wasn't going to miss an opportunity to give her the "disappointed mom" look. For good measure, she passed the look around the group. She laughed to herself; it was fun having a whole new audience to practice that on. Rolf was sometimes immune at this point.

"I cannot wait to try them," Gage said diplomatically.

Everyone grabbed their food and sat down to eat. Emma was a little surprised at how easily the Sheriff...er, Gage...fit in. The boys invited him to their next Inebriated Inconsistencies night where they played a drinking game to error-filled historic documentaries. It might be amusing to watch, she thought to herself. Emma braced herself against Albert's side as she felt a vision come on.

It was wintertime, it looked like there was snow outside. The boys were lounging by the television, laughing at something on the screen before taking a shot. Sam, Berkley, Ian, Albert, Rolf, and Gage were all there. Time sped up to show another night. The whole family was playing this time, even Gawain and Merri. Gawain was shouting at the television, so it must have been a horrible mistake on the show. Time skipped again and it looked like spring or summer with all the blooms and green. People were hanging out in the hammocks and watching the outdoor television.

Emma came back to the present. Doc looked down at her in concern.

"Are you alright?" he asked quietly in a concerned voice.

She nodded. "Just a happy little vision," she replied in a whisper. She did not want to disturb the conversation flowing around them. She vaguely heard Tess telling a few police-related pun jokes. Emma reached down and held Albert's hand. She smiled as she felt him kiss the top of her head. While Shaye was inside getting the coffee started, Emma began cleaning up the leftovers. She made sure to make a take-home bag for Gage. It would do him some good to have more homecooked food. She knew what a hassle it was to make food for just one. The vision showed he would be part of their little family, and this was her quiet way of letting him know he was accepted. She would work up to longer conversations with him.

Emma had finished making Albert a knitted throw blanket for Christmas and was in the process of wrapping it for tomorrow when her phone rang with a video call. Placing the phone high enough that he couldn't see what was at waist level, she pressed the answer button.

"Hello, Albert. How was your day?"

"It was fine. I'm looking forward to seeing you tomorrow for Christmas. It will be nice to have the day off as well. Shaye already asked me to bring some type of dessert, so I was thinking baklava. Does that sound good, or should I bring something else?" Doc asked, wanting Emma's opinion. He did make a delicious baklava, if he did say so himself. It was an old recipe, made from memory, although he did write it down for Shaye to add to the Clan's recipe book that she had started. Unfortunately, he didn't have a lot of groceries at the house. He had already made baklava for work, so he still had those ingredients on hand.

"That sounds delicious! I haven't had baklava in a while. When did you learn to make it?" Emma asked, curious.

"When I was still a member of the tribe, my mom used to make a recipe handed down through her family. I would help her make it sometimes. After I started spending more time with Thalia, she would teach me how her family made it. I sort of combined the two recipes to make my own. I don't make it a lot, since I have been the only one around to eat it; but I do make several batches at Christmas. I wrap them individually for the clinic, my version of the Christmas cookie or candy jar. I already made Sherri her own batch, which she requires each year, or she gets mad at me. It won't take me more than a couple of hours to get a large batch ready for tomorrow."

"I would love to try it. Everyone was going to get together for a little bit this evening for Christmas Eve. Will you have enough time to make the baklava and stop over tonight? Between Tess and Sam being out of town, Sam recovering, and everything else, I forgot about the ornament tree. I thought it would be fun to put out tonight. I still have a few small things to stick in their stockings but thought we could all do the little tree together. Tomorrow's plan is that we will get started early on meal prep so that we can relax later in the day. I think Sam and Berkley are making breakfast and then dinner prep will start."

"I'll come tonight and get up early to make baklava before I come over for breakfast. Feel free to put me to work tomorrow," he joked. "Did Gage ever get back to you on coming over for dinner?"

Emma nodded. "He said Christmas Eve and Day were terribly busy days, so he was going to be at work, but he was sad to miss it. I thought we could send some food over, so at least he has something homemade to eat."

"That sounds like a good plan. I'm sure he would appreciate it. It will be quite the crazy plate with the variety of foods being served."

"It will, but at least there should be something he likes!" Emma laughed.

"True enough. I'm going to finish wrapping the gifts and

I'll bring them over before dinner. Do you need me to pick anything up before I leave?" Doc asked.

"No, I think the girls and I bought out the grocery store," she replied, laughing. "Just bring your handsome self."

"Alright, I'll be over in a little bit," Doc replied. He was eager to see what everyone thought of the ornament tree. He was sure they were going to love it. Each ornament they had bought was a great representation of their family. Emma had the teacup, Doc a stethoscope, Rolf was getting the Clan crest, Shaye a coffee cup, Tess a tiny wreath of protective and healing crystals, Sam a wolf, Ian an anvil, Berkley a potter's wheel, Merri a stack of books, and Gawain had a falcon. He was looking forward to adding more when their family grew. He had a feeling Gage would be joining them eventually and had bought a Sheriff's star to have on hand. Emma had called Tim and had ordered a few extra ornaments based on what her visions had shown her, telling Doc that she would keep them until they were needed.

Christmas Day dawned bright with a dusting of snow. Emma loved how it looked and couldn't wait until the first big snowfall. She wanted to make a snowman. As everyone slowly trickled into the kitchen, Emma started the tea kettle and the coffee pot. Albert would be coming over soon for breakfast. She wondered if she might be able to sneak a baklava when he got there, for quality control purposes of course. Dinner sounded like it was going to be wonderful, but with baklava, the trifle she was making, Ian's mince pies, the cheesecake and cookies Shaye was making, Emma thought she would save most of her stomach room for dessert.

Gawain and Merri were still upstairs doing research for his next dig. Emma was not convinced that they had even gone to sleep from the day before yet. She needed to talk to

Ian and see if he would be willing to run the dinner plate in for Gage later today. Albert called out a hello from the front door, and suddenly the huge kitchen seemed happier as he came in and gave her a kiss on the top of her head.

"Why do you guys celebrate Christmas if you believe in Fate?" Shaye asked suddenly.

"All paranormals do believe in Fate. Depending on where they live, some may celebrate Christmas, Kwanza, Passover, and so on. If we live near humans, which at this point many of us do, we try our best to fit in with the local human community, so we celebrate the local customs. Christmas is a cheery holiday with happy decorations and an emphasis on spending time with family, so it is a holiday that a lot of para-normals adopted."

"Ah, okay. It just popped into my head this morning," Shaye explained.

"It's also nice because it forces all of us to reconnect at least once a year. When you live for a long time, it's easy to think 'I will get to it later, I have time,' or to just drift around the world, or to get caught up in a project that caught your interest," Emma added. "Rolf and I were the exception when it came to staying in touch. I knew people who only got in touch with family once every ten years or so, sometimes even less. Babies always draw people together, but paranormals do not get pregnant easily or often, so that can be a very long time between visits. I'm glad that we have the Clan now, since it will give everyone a home to stay at, or to come back to from traveling. We will not lose each other."

Christmas Day proceeded to be full of laughter as they played games, opened stockings, and ate so much food that she didn't think she would eat tomorrow. It was a wonderful day with her family. When the couples started heading off to their own rooms to privately exchange gifts, Emma lightly grabbed Albert's hand. "Stay a while," she told him. "I have a small gift for you."

She grabbed the gift box left under the tree. She'd been happy with how the blanket turned out, in the various shades of blues and greens. Sitting next to Albert on the couch, she handed him his present.

Doc was tickled. He had lots of fun playing the White Elephant game with the Clan and was going home with some wildly inappropriate mugs that he could never use at the clinic. The box Emma handed him wasn't very heavy and didn't rattle when he gently shook it. It had been many years since he received any gifts besides the ones Sherri gave him at the office for Christmas. He slowly opened the paper.

"Oh Emma. I love it," he said as he pulled out the soft blanket. She had knitted it in his favorite colors.

"I thought it would be perfect for your couch. You know when you take a nap, I mean rest your eyes, when you get home from work?" Emma gently teased him.

"It's perfect," Doc gently kissed her forehead. "I have a small gift for you as well," he said, going over to his coat. He had stored the box in his coat before he left home. He had gone back and forth on giving it to her. It wasn't new, but he thought she wouldn't mind. It had been in his possession a long time, and it was a cherished item, reminding him of the other woman who had loved him so long ago.

Emma took the small square box. It was a shiny decorative box with a simple bow on top. She could feel Albert's apprehension through their link. She gasped as she opened the gift. "Albert! It's gorgeous," she exclaimed. The bracelet was finely detailed and felt well loved. "Tell me about it?" Emma asked; she could tell there was history here. She looked closely at the bracelet, noticing the filigree silver inlay, the gemstones placed along the square knot design.

"It was Thalia's. Her mother gave it to her when she was young. When I left, she gave it to me and told me to give it to my mate when I found her. It's gold with some silver inlay. It has a few gemstones, but the main feature is the Herakles knot. Thalia had it because we associated it with healing. But it is also known as a love knot, supposed to represent undying commitment and love. I wanted you to have it, so you would always be able to see how I feel about you. I know it's not new—" Doc started to say before Emma pressed a finger to his mouth.

"Shush. I love that I have your mother's bracelet. And yes, I know she wasn't your birth mother," she said as Doc raised his eyebrows. "But she was the one to raise you, to teach you, protect and love you. That makes her your mother. Put it on me?" Emma asked, holding out her left arm. She wanted it to tie into her human heritage of a wedding ring on the left hand. She was grateful Fate had given her such a wonderful, gentle man. She leaned forward and pressed her lips to his. As his lips softened under hers and she felt a hand loosely grasp her hip, she climbed into his lap and felt daring enough to slide her tongue into his mouth. The groan Albert let out when her tongue tangled with his was amazing. She ran her fingers into his hair and pulled him a little closer. Her breasts felt tingly, her nipples hard. Emma was startled to realize that her womanly parts were stirring; she could feel a slight heaviness down below, a moisture that she wasn't used to feeling. This was lust, sexual attraction, something she had not felt in almost two hundred years. She wanted more of it. Emma rocked her hips against Albert, her body feeling restless. Oh my, she thought as she gasped. The friction felt wonderful against her clitoris. Emma experimentally rubbed a little more firmly against Albert; she could feel the hard length of his penis underneath her, but for once she wasn't afraid. She knew Albert would never hurt her.

Doc lightly grasped Emma's hips, encouraging her to use his body to gain pleasure. He loved that she felt comfortable enough with him to try this. Taking a deep breath, he could smell the intoxicating scent of her arousal. His tongue twined around hers, the slight roughness of their tastebuds rasping together bringing him pleasure.

"Oh, Albert, I had no idea," Emma whispered, her voice husky with desire. "This feels so…wonderful…uhn…exciting…I need…something, please," Emma pleaded. She had no idea what she needed, but the pleasure and pressure were building, and she couldn't reach the last bit.

"Do you trust me?" Doc whispered. He was pretty sure everyone in the house would stay upstairs, but just in case, he was trying to be quiet. His cock was so hard right now he could feel precum moistening his boxers, but he would take care of that later. Right now, in this heady moment, he wanted to show his mate what pleasure could feel like.

Emma nodded, still grinding her hips against his. She startled for a moment when Albert unsnapped the button on her jeans and lowered the zipper. She looked into his gaze, finding nothing but love, pleasure, and passion.

"Hold still for me for just a moment," Doc instructed. He slid his finger down into her pants, finding the curls of her mons. Feeling her plump lips, damp with her desire, he moved slowly, his finger grazing her clitoris. Drawing another deep breath, he couldn't wait until the day when he could taste her. "Tell me what feels good so I can make you fly." Doc waited for her nod until he moved, rubbing his finger gently against her clitoris.

Emma moaned, her voice pitching high into a whine. Oh goodness, she had never felt anything this amazing. Her vagina was leaking fluid, her nipples sensitive to the touch when she leaned forward to gently press a kiss on Albert's lips. His finger was rubbing small circles on her clit, his other hand pressing her hips firmly against his groin. The friction from his hard dick, combined with the roughness of his finger had her whimpering again. She was so close to something marvelous; it was just out of reach. Albert moved one arm to wrap around her back, pulling her firmly into him, her breasts smashing against his chest, his tongue seeking hers, that finger still rubbing and causing sparks of pleasure to shoot through her. That, that was what she needed, she thought as she grabbed onto his hair. His tongue slid along hers, rubbing and twisting. Emma let out a muted scream against his lips as her body burst into stars, pleasure surging through her as he pressed a little more firmly on her clit.

Doc focused on his breathing, keeping his muscles locked tight so that he wouldn't rut against her. His cock was so hard he almost came from Emma's scent and sounds alone. As he felt her body relax against his, he gently pulled his finger free, being careful not to overstimulate her. He allowed himself to indulge and sucked her juices off his finger. Looking down, he saw Emma watching him.

"You taste delicious, *agape mou*," Doc told her.

Emma leaned forward, pressing her mouth gently to his, tasting herself on his tongue. "Thank you, Albert. That was amazing," Emma said softly. She could feel his rigid length under her. "What about you?"

"I am fine," Doc assured her. "This was for you." He had no need to rush things, he wanted her to feel safe and to fully trust him when they finally came together. He had the chance to spend an eternity with his mate, waiting a few months wasn't that much time.

They snuggled for a little longer before Doc bid her goodnight.

12

It was New Year's Eve and Emma was waiting impatiently to see the town's fireworks. Sam had also bought some to set off in the backyard, as well as some sparklers. Emma laughed as the girls ran around spelling things and drawing shapes in the air with the flames. Merri and Gawain returned home, and everyone had pitched in to get Merri moved in. Emma was glad the upstairs tower room was going to get a new life as their library office. After getting all her things sorted, they had gathered for dinner and an early game night. Ian had instituted a weekly Sunday game night, and it had been a lot of fun so far. Sometimes it was the only time they were able to gather in the same place due to all their different schedules.

As midnight approached, everyone paired off for their kiss. Albert slowly leaned down and gave her a gentle kiss on her lips. "Happy New Year, my dear."

Emma started to lean in for another kiss but was stopped by Ian running up to give them both a kiss on the cheek. "Happy New Year, family," Ian said before running off to get the rest of the Clan. Emma giggled as she watched him. Merri stepped up to Rolf. "I'm ready now. Pledging to the Clan is a great way to start a new year."

There was silence while they watched Merri and Rolf face each other. Rolf bit into Merri's neck, taking a sip of her blood. Seconds later, they could all feel another presence along the Clan bond. Shaye brought over champagne glasses as they all celebrated their newest member.

When the fire diminished to only embers, they headed inside, but Ian stopped them all in the kitchen.

"This has been the best New Year's I hae had in a long time. I am so glad ye called me home," Ian said to Shaye and Tess. "It made me realize that I hae no' seen my family in a long time. Berkley and I are going to travel back to Scotland and visit. I want to introduce my mate to Mam and Da'. We are thinking about a week-long visit. Da' has a forge at the farm, and I want to see how he has it set up, maybe get some ideas for our workshop."

"I want to go," Shaye pouted. "I haven't seen your parents in forever. When did they move back to Scotland?"

Ian looked sheepish. "Weel…"

Emma could only shake her head as Ian went on to explain that the "parents" Shaye knew were really his aunt and uncle. His real parents were in Scotland. When he came over to the US to create a new identity, his aunt and uncle acted as his parents for the paper trail. When Tess smacked the back of his head for forgetting to tell Shaye that little tidbit, Emma kind of agreed with her.

"Group hug," Emma declared. She wanted her kids to make up; she wanted this fresh new year to start with only positive things to hopefully set the tone for the whole year. She took a moment to bask in the feeling of her family surrounding her. She never would have guessed this would be her life even a year ago. As everyone said good night and headed to their own rooms, Emma leaned up on her toes to whisper in Albert's ear. "Can we go to your house tonight?"

He glanced down at her, surprise on his face. "Of course. Did you want to drive or walk over?"

"Let's walk. It's a gorgeous clear night out," Emma suggested. She thought a stroll under the stars sounded romantic.

Albert held out her coat for her to put on and then held open the front door. She took her key out and locked up behind them. Since she had always stayed the night at the house, she sent a quick text to her son that she would be out tonight.

'Eww, Mom. I didn't want to know, but thanks for making sure I don't worry. You okay?' Rolf asked.

'I'm wonderful. I just didn't want you to panic if I wasn't there in the morning.'

'Okay. Night, Mom. Love you.'

'Love you too,' Emma responded before shutting the link down.

Emma took Albert's hand as they walked down the driveway. "Do you think anyone will ever beat you in *Ticket To Ride*?" she asked teasingly. It was one of the games they had played tonight, and Albert won most of the games. Sam seemed determined to beat him though, which was funny since he was usually laid back about winning.

Doc laughed. "I only have two games on my phone. It was my way of relaxing after work before I started hanging out at the Clan house. I've really enjoyed these game nights though. It was a good idea."

She nodded. "I'm glad Ian suggested it. I never would have played half the games we have tried."

"Did you get to call Samantha and Douglas for the New Year?" Doc asked.

"I did. I called them this morning. They're doing well. Their youngest brought home a baby goat, so they've been busy with the new addition."

"That sounds exciting. I'm a little surprised none of our

kids have a pet yet. Shaye and Tess couldn't stop talking about the animals they saw at the pumpkin patch's petting zoo," Doc responded.

"I think they'll get some eventually. They all seem like pet people."

"What about you? Do you want any pets of your own?" Doc asked.

"I think so. It's been a while since I've had a fun pet; all the animals I had at the farm had a double purpose. The cows gave milk that we used to make cheese and butter. The goats gave milk and wool. Chickens for meat and eggs. Even the horses had another job. Do you like pets?" Emma replied, questioningly.

"I do. Likewise, it has been a very long time since I had one, and most of them were working animals. I think my last one was a horse to get around town, if that tells you anything." He laughed. "I had a turtle one time since they live so long. We didn't really do much though, I would sit in the grass and let him eat and wander around. It would be nice to have a pet to be able to do something fun with."

"Maybe we can look into getting a house pet," Emma suggested.

"That sounds like a good idea," Doc agreed as they reached his house. "Would you like some tea?" he asked as they walked in.

"I had something else in mind," Emma said, attempting to flirt.

"I have water or some wine, if that sounds better?" Doc asked, opening the refrigerator to see what else he had available. "I think I have a juice…" he trailed off as she gently pushed the door shut.

"Albert… It's a new year and I…" Emma was not brought up to be so blatant about sexual desires. After Vlad, she had never had an interest in anything sexual, so she wasn't sure how to go about this.

"Yes?" Doc encouraged.

"You've been so patient with me. I would love to start this new year out as your mate."

"You already are my mate, *agapi mou*," Doc responded, not sure what she was trying to say, but wanting to be supportive.

"Yes, that's true. But I want to be your mate. Officially," Emma responded, stressing the last word, her cheeks blazing.

"Oh! Right. Yes. I understand," Doc stammered, his own cheeks heating a bit as he realized what she was trying to say. "Are you sure? I don't want to push you." He told his beast to shut up when it tried to lodge a protest.

"I'm sure." Emma smiled as she leaned forward to press a kiss to his lips.

Doc took her hand, kissing her knuckles, before leading her to his room. He had a king-sized bed and he was grateful he had spent last night cleaning. The sheets were new and he didn't have laundry everywhere. He dimmed the lights, trying to get a romantic feel.

"I might need to go slow, if that is okay. I haven't had any experience other than...anyway, I'm not sure what to do or what might trigger—" Emma paused.

"I am fine with taking it slow. I have an idea that might help; what if you were on top? You would have more control," Doc suggested.

Emma nodded, her heart racing. She wanted to belong to Albert, she just had to fight her anxiety to get it. She leaned forward, placing a kiss on his lips. She groaned as his arms wrapped around her and his tongue plundered her mouth gently. Albert walked them over to his bed, kissing her as they went. He sat on the edge, and she bent to follow his mouth. Kissing him was addictive. She moved her shaking hands to unbutton his shirt. Even dressed casually, he wore a long-sleeve button-down shirt with his jeans. As the buttons came undone, she saw his chest hair poking out. Not enough to be furry, but enough for her to run her fingers through and to grab. His nipples pebbled in the cooler air, and she didn't stop herself from leaning down to taste those as well. She gave one a gentle nibble, moving to the other one when Albert moaned quietly.

Doc moved his hands to her sweater. "May I?" he asked, his hands on the bottom hem. Emma hesitated for a moment. At her nod, he slowly inched the shirt up, kissing as he went. When she raised her arms, he pulled the sweater completely off. Emma had on a lacy bra, her breasts pert and looking delicious. Doc could see a vicious-looking scar at the curve of her shoulder and neck. He could only imagine it came from Vlad's attack. He had never noticed it before; the shirts she wore didn't show that area. Ignoring it for now, he knew she would be self-conscious. He ran a finger along the edge of the bra, keeping an eye on her responses, loving how she shivered, the scent of her arousal becoming stronger. He reached behind her to unsnap her bra, her breasts falling into his face as he released them. Doc traced the edge of the nipple with his tongue, listening to her quick inhale. He could hear her heart racing and glanced up at her.

"More," Emma demanded, pushing his head back down to her breasts. She never knew they were so sensitive. Her cheeks flamed as she heard Albert's quiet chuckle.

"Yes, my dear," he responded before placing her entire nipple in his mouth. Gently sucking on the hardened nub, he reached down to unzip her pants, easing his finger in to play with her lips.

Emma moaned softly as Albert found her clit, her vagina responding by soaking his fingers. She had no idea it could feel this good. Emma grabbed his hair, pulling him even closer. She wanted to feel his body against hers. He had toned muscles, a light six-pack showing as she pushed his shirt off his shoulders. His body was muscled, but it was a lean muscle build, not too bulky. His shoulders were broader, his sculpted chest glistening with the light bouncing off his white hairs. His torso tapered down to his hips, a V leading down to his groin. Emma suddenly wanted to see where that V went. She gently pushed Albert back onto the bed. Once he was lying down, she ran her fingertips over his pecs, playing with his nipples before trailing them down his abs. His muscles tensed and he huffed out a laugh. "A little ticklish," he explained. Emma lightly scraped her fingernails over the muscles, erasing the ticklish feeling. His hips were calling to her, that V drawing her in, making her want to explore. She glanced up at him with her hand on his pants.

Doc nodded. "I'm yours," he said. "Explore if you want to."

Emma quickly smiled at him before concentrating on her task again. Carefully lowering his zipper, she pulled the edges of his pants away, revealing the edge of his underwear. When Albert lifted his hips off the bed, she slid his pants completely off and tossed them aside. His royal blue briefs had quite the noticeable bulge in the front. She wasn't quite sure how to tackle that yet, but she wanted to try. For now, she traced her hands down his hips to feel the texture on his legs. His hair was white even here, coarse against her hands. Albert's breaths were coming harsher now, his eyes watching her. Moving back up to his hips, she drew the briefs down and watched as his cock popped up to smack him in the stomach. He was an intimidating size, probably six and a half inches, girthy. And uncircumcised. Emma wrapped her hands around it, barely able to close her fingers. Only her thumb and middle finger touched at all. Albert sharply inhaled as her hand caressed his penis, the head poking out as she moved her hand around, manipulating the foreskin.

"Tell me how to make it feel good," Emma told him. He made her feel amazing and she wanted to do the same for him.

"You can grip a little tighter," Doc said through gritted teeth. He didn't want to come yet; he was enjoying the experience of his mate exploring his body. "Squeeze a little more when you get to the top of the head. You can play with the foreskin."

Emma grasped him a little tighter, squeezing when she reached the top. She let her other hand drift down to play with his testicles, feeling them draw up tighter against his body. Emma experimented with how tight to squeeze his cock, listening to his breathing, trying to capture the moans.

After several minutes of strokes, Doc reached down and gently stilled her hand. "I don't want to come yet," he explained. It had been an incredibly long time since he had been intimate with another person. Like a hundred years or more long time. His body was primed to go, but he wanted to let Emma set the pace as much as possible. "Come up here, my love," Doc said as he scooted farther up the bed. He wanted to keep Emma on top as much as possible, giving her control of her position.

Emma quickly shed her pants before pausing at her underwear. Albert was lying there, muscled body on display, a light sheen of sweat along his body. Emma took a deep breath and slid her underwear down as well.

Doc groaned as he watched his sexy mate slide her underwear down her shapely legs. He really was a beast, wanting to lick and bite along her whole body. She wasn't ready for that though. "May I taste you?" Doc asked, wanting to taste the juices he had been smelling. As Emma nodded shyly, he patted his chest. "Come straddle me," he instructed, with an encouraging smile.

Emma looked down at her mate incredulously. When he patted his chest again, she gingerly threw a leg over his chest to straddle him. She started scooting up, bracing a hand on the headboard. Even as he motioned to come closer, she stopped. "Are you sure I won't suffocate you? I'm literally on your chest and you're going to be surrounded by me."

"I'll be fine, *agapi mou*. Let me have a taste," Doc told her. He was desperate to see if she tasted as good as she smelled.

Emma finished scooting the last inch or so to his face. Albert closed his eyes, drew in a deep breath, and let out a moan so deep she could feel it vibrate in his chest below her. His hands gently clasped her hips, and she jolted a moment later when she felt his tongue touch her. He traced the old scars on the interior of her thighs, moving upwards to reach her vagina. She could feel her face burning hot as she looked down at her mate. Her pubis was right in front of his face, it was incredibly intimate. His tongue was a little rough in texture, a little wet, gliding over her lips, teasing them open. Reaching her clit, he rubbed small circles around it before finally licking it in one broad lick. "More, Albert," Emma pleaded. It felt so good. She felt his arm move, reaching behind her. His fingers began lightly stroking her lips as he started to suck on her clit. The sensations were like nothing she had ever experience before and she craved more. He lapped from the bottom of her opening all the way to her clit, his tongue wiggling gently as he went. She tensed again briefly when she felt a finger slide into her folds. As his finger began to thrust into her, his tongue applied a little more pressure, pleasure bursting through her, causing her to lean forward even more, chasing the feel of his tongue. She barely noticed when he added a second finger, just a fuller sensation. His finger bent slightly inside her, hitting what had to be her G-spot. After a few thrusts against that magic spot, her climax tore through her. The pleasure so intense that her vision whited out for a second. When she could catch her breath, she was mortified when she realized her vagina had leaked a lot of fluid. She was sure she had soaked his face. Oh lord, how could she have done that? she thought to herself. What was that?

She tried backing down his chest, her cheeks red with mortification.

Doc held her in place. "What's wrong?"

"I…uh…I…got you wet," Emma whispered, mortified.

Doc just hummed, pressing his mouth against her clit once more. Giving her one last long firm lick, he looked her in the eyes. "That is the best compliment you can give me, *agapi mou*, my love. That I gave you pleasure, that you trusted me and that your body enjoyed it so thoroughly, makes me feel good. I want to make you happy, protect you, please you. That extra wetness may not happen every time, but it is a wonderful thing. Did you want to stop for tonight? We can just cuddle, watch a show, or go to sleep. I can take you home too if you need a break," he offered. He didn't want to pressure her to stay if she needed time to adjust. He could take care of himself when he was alone, if that was what she wanted. The memory of her squirting on him would bring him to climax quickly.

"It's okay? Really?" Emma asked, her body still buzzing with pleasure.

"Completely. I can't wait to find other ways to make you orgasm that hard." Doc smiled at her.

Emma couldn't sense a lie. His smile set her at ease, as did the hard evidence pressing into her backside. His cock was still full, still hard, so he must have enjoyed it.

"I want to stay. Can we keep going?" she asked, wanting to feel his length inside her. She was ready to be his mate, officially. Even with the longer (or, you know, forever) lifespan, she felt confident in her decision. There was a way to offer the immortality to her family, and it would then be up to them to decide.

Doc reached up to gently caress her cheek. "We can, if you want to."

"How do alicorns mate?" Emma asked. "We need to be intimate when I say the vow. Rolf did his mentally, but I'm not sure if that's a requirement or not."

"I'm not entirely sure. I'm hoping my beast will guide me.

I haven't run across another one of my kind to ask. Most shifters bite or mark in some way, but I'm not sure if I'll bite since my animal is an herbivore. If I have the urge to bite, I'll try to warn you," Doc offered. He saw the scarring on her neck, knew she had a traumatic experience with bites before and didn't want to trigger that during their mating night.

Emma rocked backward a little, wanting to feel his cock against her body again. She absently reached behind her to slowly stroke him, wanting to have that connection while she responded.

"That last time with Vlad, he wasn't gentle in trying to kill me. He didn't quite tear out my throat, but I had bites in lots of places and the spot on my shoulder was missing a rather large chunk. When Rolf saved me, the smaller bites healed well enough that you can't notice them now. The shoulder one healed, but as you can see it is ugly, it never really disappeared."

Doc interrupted her. "It's not ugly. Yes, it's a scar. Yes, it was a horrible thing to happen to you. But you survived, that's what the scar tells me. It tells me you are a survivor and a fighter. It shows me just how grateful I need to be that you are here with me; you could have died before I even met you. I love this mark," he informed her as he sat up to place a kiss on it.

"Can you bite me there, if you need to bite? I want a happy mark to take its place," Emma requested.

"I will. You can bite me too," Doc offered. He wanted Emma to bite him, to permanently wear her mark. The primal part of his brain wanted to be the one to feed her.

Emma leaned forward, pressing her lips gently to Albert's. Running her fingers through his hair, loving that it was even a little coarse in his human form, she grabbed a handful and pulled his face closer to hers. She let out a sigh of relief when his arms wrapped around her back, holding her tight. His hard cock was still pressed against her, and she desperately wanted to know what it felt like inside her. His tongue dove into her mouth, tangling with hers before kissing his way down her neck, to suckle on her breasts. Her nipples hardened under the tongue lashing and she mewed as he gently sucked them into his mouth. As her vagina got wetter, she started rubbing against his body, his pubic hair tickling her clitoris in the best of ways. Albert reached down to slide a finger into her opening, her vaginal muscles clenching around it, trying to pull him in deeper. When he slid a second finger in, she started shaking. "Please, love. Let me have you, I need more. I need to feel you."

"Sit up a little bit and I'll help guide it in. If it hurts, tell me and we'll stop and stretch you out a little bit more, work up to three fingers maybe." Doc's cock was so hard he thought he would burst as soon as he got inside her wet heat. He lightly flicked the tip of his dick to calm it the heck down before helping her ease her way onto his shaft. The enveloping warmth and heat, combined with her clenching muscles, almost made him come as soon as he was fully seated. Gritting his teeth, he stroked his hands down his lover's back, wanting her to feel good all over.

"Kiss me, Albert. I'm ready," Emma told him. She felt so full, his cock rubbing along her inner walls, her vagina leaking more fluid allowing him to thrust smoothly. Her nipples sensitive, she moaned as she grazed them along his chest hair when she leaned in to kiss him. As his tongue danced with hers, she couldn't keep her hips still, grinding down on his shaft, rubbing her clit against his pubic hair, loving how his balls bounced against her ass when she changed from grinding to bouncing. Leaning down, she bit his nipples.

Doc gasped. His beast coming up to join him. *Yes, bite again*, his beast wanted. *Pretty mate.* Doc was stunned when Emma reached back and fondled his balls. Oh goodness, that was... He nibbled on her bottom lip, moving down to suck on her breasts. Angling his hips, he changed his thrusts to hit her G-spot, wanting to make her fly.

Emma bit down hard on his nipple, causing him to thrust hard up into her welcoming heat as he felt her teeth enter him. His dick felt like it was getting massaged as he felt her climax rush through her. "Drink, love," he begged her hoarsely. *Bite, make ours*, his beast demanded. "Gonna bite," he warned, feeling his climax barrel through him.

Emma lifted her head, licking the bites closed. Turning her head to give him her neck, she bit down on him again, their teeth breaking skin at the same time.

"I take you, Albert, as my Mate. To love and cherish forevermore," Emma spoke telepathically. Her mouth was otherwise occupied. Goodness, he tasted delicious.

"I take you, Emmaline, as my Mate. To love and cherish forevermore," Doc replied, a little surprised he could speak to her without the Clan bond. His beast rose up and claimed Emma as well. *Mine.*

"Yes, yours too. And you are mine," Emma reassured the beast.

As soon as she confirmed the bond with both sides of Albert, their bond snapped into place, a golden glow enveloping them. She could feel energy surging through her, changing her. She felt vitalized; she didn't think it was just from the mate bond as she hadn't heard of anyone else glowing.

Mine now. Ours. Forever. Emma heard Albert's beast state contently.

"Does that mean I'm immortal now?" Emma asked. She watched as Doc spoke silently to his beast.

"He says yes. I'm still not sure how to initiate the bond with the rest of the Clan. I tried to reach out through the forum, but I haven't heard back yet. I am hoping I hear something before Ian and Berkley leave. It would be nice for them to have a little more protection when they are far away from us."

Emma leaned forward to press a kiss to his cheek. "I'll help you look," she replied. "After we get a shower though," she added, wrinkling her nose slightly. She could feel his cum beginning to leak out of her.

Doc laughed. "A shower sounds good. Maybe a cup of tea too."

13

Emma woke, held tight in her Albert's arms. They had been alternating between sleeping at his house and her room in the Clan house this week. Today though, the Clan was helping them move most of his things to her room. There were a few changes of clothes being left behind because you never knew how a day at the clinic would go. Albert had been thrown up on more than once. The bed was also staying because she already had one at the house, and it would be a good place to stay if they wanted a night away from everyone. He was also leaving his backup tea pot and a few kitchen items. Emma was happy he was bringing the jade teapot though; she had happy memories of sharing tea and learning about her mate over that teapot.

"Hmm," Albert hummed. "Good morning, my dear. What time is it?"

"We have about a half an hour before people start showing up," Emma replied, stretching, and subtly rubbing her cheeks against his groin. After a couple of gentle rubs, she could feel his shaft growing and hardening against her. She grinned, loving how he burrowed his nose in her hair and took a deep breath before kissing her on her neck. He made sure to kiss there at least once a day, making her feel loved and protected. It was like a little promise just between the two of them.

"We should hurry then," Doc replied, sliding his hand down to cup her mons, chuckling as her hips rotated against him impatiently. Emma was coming into her own and it was delightful to see, not to mention arousing. She was getting more comfortable initiating and although they kept to positions with her on top, he was thoroughly enjoying the experience.

"Yes, please," Emma breathed, reaching behind her to grab his hair. She gripped tight as his finger slid between her lips, teasing her clit. She was already wet for him; she had woken up aroused from spending the night in his arms, breathing in his scent. It didn't hurt that they both slept naked last night, so she had felt his bare skin against hers all night long. The touch between her legs got a little firmer, his finger rubbing circles on her clit before sliding down to tease her entrance. His cock nestled in between her butt cheeks as he rocked into her. She could probably come like this, but she really wanted to feel him deep inside her. Spreading her legs, she arched further back, his cockhead grazing her taint.

Letting go of his hair, she pressed his hand firmly between her legs and arched her back to bring her entrance in line with his cock. Pushing her hips out, her breath caught as he slid inside her. All silken hardness, his cock was so hard and thick that he stretched her almost to the point of discomfort. Focusing on the way his dick rubbed against her walls, creating delicious friction, and the way his finger was still playing with her clitoris, she felt her body adjust and let him all the way inside. Once he was fully seated, she slowly thrust her hips, loving the drag of his shaft against her walls. Emma tried to maintain a rhythm but kept being distracted whenever his finger grazed the perfect spot, or his cock hit inside of her just right.

'*Please, Albert,*' she pleaded after losing the rhythm again, frustrated. She needed to feel his cock stroking inside her, needed the sensation of being stuffed full, of being cared for.

"You want me to take over?" he asked. At her nod, Doc adjusted his positioning without leaving her body. His right arm moved underneath her to massage her nub, his left hand grasped her hip, keeping her close to his body. He started thrusting, slow and deep for a few times before increasing his speed. He knew he hit the jackpot when her breathing caught in a little moan, the breathy sound shooting straight to his balls, making them draw up. He didn't want to come before her, so he threw a leg over her hips to help him stay inside her as he continued to thrust, moving his hand to her breasts, pinching and rolling the nipples in the way she liked.

Kissing her neck, he let his beast merge a little bit and began to pound gently into her warm welcoming body.

Emma was awash in pleasure, tucked in safely against her mate, she felt like she was flying. The position allowed him to hold her snuggly but didn't make her feel trapped. She felt impaled on his thrusting length, his cock hitting her G-spot with every thrust, the drag of his dick against her walls sending her into a constant stream of pleasure. She was almost there. '*Please,*' she pleaded, needing something to throw her over the edge.

'*Eat, my dear. Eat while I make you mine again,*' she heard Albert say before his arm moved in front of her face. Grabbing his wrist, she bit deeply, swallowing his delicious flavor, she let go on a scream as he gave one final hard thrust, while gently pinching her clit. As her vision grayed out on the edges, she felt his warmth spread inside her as he climaxed as well. Licking the marks closed, she snuggled back, eager to keep his dick inside of her for a moment longer. She enjoyed feeling this close to him.

'*Mom. I really hope I'm not interrupting, but we're on our way down. Just don't be naked when we come in. ETA ten minutes,'* she heard Rolf say in her mind.

Smiling, Emma looked over her shoulder at Albert. *'The kids are on their way and Rolf requested we not be naked when they arrive.'*

"Prudes," Doc chuckled. "We better grab a quick shower then." Caressing her one last time, he gently pulled out. Holding out a hand, he helped her stand. "We can save time if we share the shower," he suggested.

Emma laughed at him, knowing it wouldn't save any time, but followed him anyway. Just as they were getting out and drying off, they heard a knock on the door.

Doc threw on some clothes and rushed out of their room. "I'll let them in and get coffee going and the kettle on for tea. Did you want anything for breakfast?"

"I think we still have some muffins. I'll just grab one of those," Emma said, giving him a kiss before shutting the door so she could get ready without flashing the kids when they came in.

Humming happily, she dressed in comfortable clothes, not caring that her hair was a wet mess still. She just threw it into a ponytail and walked out to meet her family. Hearing voices and laughter, she followed the sound into the kitchen.

"What all are we bringing back to the Clan house?" Ian asked, grabbing a donut from the bakery box they must have brought.

"The boxes in the front room, which are mostly kitchen and my clothes. I have some medical supplies I wanted to bring to restock the house as well. I was wondering if I could use one of the rooms as an office? The times you guys have been hurt, we have treated at the house, so I thought it would be good to have a room there. I have a lot of books I wouldn't want to leave here either. I have protections here, but I would feel better if they were at the Clan house. There's better protection and almost always someone there," Doc explained.

The books he was most worried about were the extremely rare ones that Thalia had given him and other ones he had collected for hundreds of years.

"That's a good idea," Rolf responded. He wanted to make sure Doc felt welcomed, both as a Clan member and as his mother's mate. "There's a small room in the tower that is open on the second floor. The basement has space, or the left side of the house has a few open rooms. On the backside of the house, on the main floor, there is my office and what I keep meaning to make into a theater room. In the front of the house, main floor, we have a pretty big space as well; I just have some knickknack type of things in there now, but those are easily moved. I should probably clean those out anyway; I don't even remember what is in there." It was a bunch of stuff from his travels, but most were in boxes. They could easily get sent to the basement for storage, or if he found something really neat when he sorted through them, Rolf figured he could find space in his office or the library. He should probably sort through the basement and make shelves for everyone to keep their things. The house was big, but he was sure they all had stuff, or would have stuff in the future, that they wanted to keep. If everyone had a space in the basement, it would help. He should really redo the bedroom that was down there too.

"Rolf?" Shaye nudged him.

"Sorry, I went down a rabbit hole of what should be done in the basement. I was thinking I need to convert the bedroom into bunkbeds so we can all fit. It's a panic room slash storm shelter. I may need to get rid of the exercise room down there and expand the storm shelter area, so we aren't so cramped if we ever need to use it. I want to get more shelves and organize the storage area so everyone can have their own space. Anyway, back to what we were talking about, Doc's office."

"I think putting it on the main floor makes sense, that way we don't have to carry anyone up the stairs if we have any more injuries. I think I would prefer it to be in the back of the house though, if that's possible," Doc replied. Not that anyone would be in the room for long with all of their increased healing, but if it was in the back of the house, there should be less noise and foot traffic going by the room so the person could heal in peace. They generally were not loud, but if they were all in the kitchen or living room, it could get a little noisy.

"Shouldn't be a problem. I've had that space cleared out for a theater but never actually got started. I'll call in some contractors that I know and have them come look at the space. Feel free to tell them what you want where, or make a list or layout, so it's what you need. They can work on the theater room when they're done with that. I think we would have lots of fun having a movie room," Rolf replied.

"Thank you. I would feel better having the books and supplies there. I can just store them in our room for now until the construction is done." Doc felt some relief that he would be able to keep his collection close.

They drove caravan-style back to the house and everyone helped unload. Even Gawain took a break to help.

"How many boxes of books do you have, Doc?" Ian asked, his arms stacked high with boxes.

"A few." Doc laughed.

It was nice having so many paranormals in the house, Emma thought. It made moving much easier since they could move heavier loads without a problem. When the last boxes were stored away, Shaye ordered pizza for lunch. Everyone ate and talked, the air filled with happy noise. Once everyone had eaten their fill, Rolf looked around the kitchen.

"What do you think of having a celebratory run since everyone is now moved in? Non-runners could walk or just hang out outside?" Rolf suggested. He knew Tess and Shaye didn't really run with the group since they didn't have a faster form. He thought Merri would probably stay behind too.

Doc looked over at Emma, a question on his face. She shrugged; it really was up to him when to disclose his animal, although she thought the kids would love to see it. *'It's up to you, Albert,'* Emma told him. *'Maybe Berkley can adjust your pendant and conceal your animal so you can run around the property. It would be nice for you to be able to stretch your wings out finally.'*

'Do you think it is alright if I don't tell them about the immortality thing yet? I still don't have a clear answer on how to share it with them, and I'd like to be able to have solid information to give them when I present the option,' Doc questioned uncertainly.

'I think that is a fine plan,' Emma reassured him, moving over to hold his hand.

"I would love to run with you, but I have to tell you about my animal first," Doc said. "Berkley, is there a way to hide my animal from everyone but the Clan? I know it seems silly, but once I shift, you'll understand. I have not shifted outside in such a long time, but I would love to run with you," he added longingly.

Berkley took a long look at him before holding out his hand. "Give me your pendant and I can modify it." He held the pendant cupped between his hands, whispering a few words and a bright light briefly flashed. Handing it back, he said, "It will hide your shifted form and scent from everyone but us. It will change shape to accommodate your size and is spelled to not fall off."

Doc slipped the pendant back on. After taking a deep breath, he raised Emma's hand to his lips, pressing a quick kiss there before taking a step back from everyone.

"It's better if I am outside. I don't want to accidently break anything in the house." His horse body was rather large and although he probably would fit in the space, he did not want to risk it. As he walked outside, he was aware of his family following him. *'Do* not *try to claim them right now,'* Doc told his beast. *'We will wait until we find out how to share our immortality with them. I think this is enough of a shock for today.'* He felt his beast humph and pout, but it didn't argue with him. Thank goodness. He had enough to worry about right at this moment. Standing in the grass next to the patio, he closed his eyes, letting his control over his beast loose and felt the change surge through him.

He heard gasps from the group and then utter silence. *'Emma? Did I shift strange or something? I don't want to look,'* he pouted. The silence was unnerving.

'No, my love. They are just in awe and a bit of shock, I think. Poor Gawain might fall over. Or orgasm. I'm not really sure what that face is he's making,' Emma tried making a dirty joke, hoping to set Albert at ease.

Doc snorted and dared to crack an eye open. Gawain really was making quite a ridiculous face. Of course, he had been searching for a unicorn tribe, and here was a partial unicorn standing in front of him. That had to be a shock.

"Um…you're…what…how are…when did…" Gawain couldn't complete his sentences, just trailing off after each start.

Shaye stepped forward. "Can I give you a hug?" she asked quietly, her hand outstretched for his beast to scent.

Mine, his beast said contentedly. *My foal.*

'She's our adopted daughter; she's not a horse,' Doc replied to his beast, nonplussed.

Still mine, was the adamant reply.

Doc focused on the girl in front of him, nodding his head. He was careful where he put his horn. The last thing he needed to do was accidentally impale someone; other than when Emma had found him, it had been years since he had shifted near anyone else. Watching as she approached slowly, he nuzzled into her hand, letting his beast catch her scent. The giggle Shaye let out when his soft muzzle tickled her hand made his soul happy.

'*See? They're going to love you,*' Emma reassured Albert. She could still sense his nervousness, although Shaye's immediate acceptance had started to soothe it.

Once Shaye approached him, the others slowly made their way over.

"Thank you for sharing this with us, Doc," Rolf said as he came over. "We'll keep it safe," he promised. The others all nodded.

After his beast had gotten the scent of all his family, they started to get ready for the run. Shaye, Tess, and Merri were going to stay back and enjoy the outdoor fireplace. Emma said she would run with the group for a little bit. She wanted to experience it and to support Albert in his first shifted run with the Clan. She wouldn't stay long since she knew they would all slow down to accommodate her and she wanted Albert to enjoy himself and stretch his legs.

Doc was happy…ecstatic…what was a word for more than happy? Feeling the wind through his mane as he ran with his family made even his beast joyful. For once, his beast wasn't pushing at him to claim them, which was good progress. Doc just hoped that it lasted a while. Once he found out more information, he would bring up claiming to the group, he promised himself. They ran for a few miles, taking a loop that crossed near the backyard again. Emma stopped, saying she was going to hang out with the girls over their Clan link. Doc ran back to nuzzle Emma before racing off to catch up with the group. When they came to a clearing in the woods, Doc decided to test his wings and join Gawain up in the air. Running, he spread out his wings and started pumping them to catch the wind. Rising up higher, he whinnied in joy as his wings spread out, pushing the air to keep him afloat. Gawain's falcon flew in close, flying by his side. As much as stretching his legs and running with his Clan brought him joy, it doubled when he was able to stretch his wings for the first time in many years. Doc stayed over the group, enjoying the feeling of community even when he was up in the air. He could see Gawain studying his movements and knew he would have lots of questions when they landed. As much as Doc wanted to keep flying, his wings were getting tired after not being used for so long. He consoled his beast that with the pendant, they would be able to fly more often, and they would soon be able to fly for longer times. Eventually, he would like to be able to take Emma for a ride.

'I'm heading back to the house,' Doc said over the Clan link. *'It's been too long since I've done this, sorry. I'll have to get my stamina back up,'* he apologized. He really was sorry to cut it short. He landed in the backyard of the house, the girls coming over to bring him a water.

"Did you have fun?" Emma asked, rubbing his neck.

Doc changed back to human before answering. "So much fun," he replied, grinning. "I need to work on my stamina though. It's been so long since I was able to take flight." He could hear footsteps coming closer and turned toward the woods. Gawain landed in the backyard just as everyone else ran in, Sam running to the side of the house to change and get his clothes on.

"Okay. I have questions," Gawain said as soon as he was human. "Alicorns are real? Seriously? How many of you are there? What about unicorns? Do you know any? How old are you? Where did you come from? Why do you shift with your clothes on?"

"Slow down and breathe, Gawain," Doc instructed. He was worried the man was going to start hyperventilating or pass out. "Let's go inside to finish the conversation; I could use another drink."

Emma went into the kitchen to get some coffee, tea, and hot chocolate started. Shaye joined her and helped create a snack tray with some fruit, nuts, pretzels, and cookies. As they walked back into the living room, everyone had found a seat and seemed to be waiting on them. Emma knew the story, but it was nice they waited.

"Alright, Gawain. Let me start answering some of your questions. Yes, I am real. Yes, I am an alicorn. As far as I know, I may be the only one. I haven't met any others. I find that most flight-based shifters can shift with their clothes on. I am not sure why it seems to be only the flying ones that have that ability.

"Originally my people were from Greece but moved here before I was born. I can still speak Greek, as that was the language that was used the most around our tribe. We left because hunters had grown in numbers, and we were constantly looking over our shoulders and having to hide our animal side." Doc took a breath.

"Tribe? What type of shifters were your parents?" Gawain asked.

Doc smiled down at her as Emma reached over and held his hand. "They were unicorns. They came over to this land before Erikson made it here. I'm not sure why I shifted differently than everyone else, but the tribe was not pleased. I was kicked out as soon as I was considered an adult. One of the elders, a healer, took me under her wing from the time I shifted until I was made to leave. She taught me about healing and helped me learn what we could about my beast. There is not a lot of information readily available about the rarer shifters. I am still trying to learn about my animal side."

"What kind of hunters?" Rolf asked, concerned. He had run across a few in his time as well. It was never a pleasant experience.

"Because we were unicorns, it was both paranormal and human hunters. Humans wanted the horns for magic and supposed healing abilities, paranormals wanted us for the same thing. Our horns aren't a source of magic though. A lot of unicorns have some sort of healing ability, so if it was a paranormal hunter, you may not be killed, only captured, and enslaved to keep them healthy. Supposedly several of our tribe had been killed or taken, thus the move across the ocean to try to find freedom. However, once more people started coming over, the rumors returned, and we were hunted again. We moved a lot, at least until the tribe started producing several foals and we settled down in one spot. Shifting was extremely restricted, most of it was behind walls or inside a large structure."

"Where was it?" Gawain asked eagerly, his scholarly thirst for knowledge springing up.

"Near Montana. You're on the right track; although, the last time I was there, there wasn't much of any buildings left," Doc cautioned. "It didn't look like they were attacked, more that they had moved on or died out. I never saw anyone I knew from the tribe again. They were very much isolationists, so it wouldn't surprise me if the tribe ended due to lack of new members."

"How old are you?" Berkley asked quietly.

"Two thousand-ish, give or take a little bit. I don't remember when my birthday actually is. I remember being told it was in the winter. My parents did not celebrate my birth."

"Well, at least I'm not the oldest one anymore," Berkley replied, trying to lighten the sadness he saw on Doc's face.

Emma joined in. "Albert picked January sixteenth for his birthday. I told him he needed to have a day so we could celebrate."

"It doesn't have to be that day. I just picked a winter month and day; I didn't want it to interfere with Christmas."

"I think that sounds like a grand idea," Ian said cheerfully. "What do ye want to do for your birthday?"

"Oh, nothing big. Plus, aren't you guys going to be going to Scotland for a visit? I haven't ever had a birthday celebration; we don't need to change anything around for it this year!" Doc protested.

Berkley glanced at Ian. "We've moved it back until February. Flights are cheaper then and it was a better time to visit his parents. Would you like to go out to eat or have something here? Ian and I can make that brisket you liked at Thanksgiving, or whatever else you might want," he offered.

Doc couldn't help the smile that came over his face. These people really were his family. He could tell that Berkley made up that story on the spot, but it meant a lot to him that they would adjust their plans for his made-up birthday. "I'd like it to be just the family at the house. Otherwise, we'll have everyone from town all over us. The brisket sounds delicious, thank you." No matter where he went in town, someone always stopped to talk to him. It was the one negative of being the only doctor. He had enjoyed it before, and still did, but it was hard to get any alone time with Emma or the family if they were out in town.

A dinner at home with his family, the family who now knew what he was, would be an amazing way to celebrate his birthday.

14

It was officially Albert's birthday tomorrow. Emma had conspired with Sherri to make sure he didn't have any visits scheduled after four o'clock tomorrow evening. Tess and Shaye were going to hang a Happy Birthday banner in the waiting room, along with balloons outside. Shaye had even found a large pin that she was going to make Albert wear as revenge for her own birthday outfit. They had found a huge card at the store, and they were hiding in the office for people to sign. Whether or not Albert wanted a fuss made, his family was going to make sure he knew how loved he was. And part of that was letting the town in on the long-held secret of his birthday.

Today though, today was just for the two of them. Emma had planned a picnic out in the park. She had most of the things packed up already. It was still cold outside and there was a fine dusting of snow on the ground, but she trusted Albert when he said he could drive into the park without a problem. Leaning over, she kissed him awake. She was surprised he slept so long, but they had been up rather late last night. Emma blushed thinking about their activities. Who knew wall sex could be so fun?

"Albert," she said softly. "Wake up, it's time for our picnic. I'm going to finish getting it ready, if you want to get dressed," Emma cajoled.

"Morning, my love. I'll be just a minute," Doc said, burrowing his head back into his pillow. This bed was so comfortable. "Ahh!" he shouted a second later as his laughing partner tore all the covers off him.

"Up and at 'em, old man. It's time to go." She laughed as she ran out the door.

"Old man, hmph," Doc grumbled. "She didn't call me old last night." Maybe he could persuade her to have some fun at their picnic. He rushed through the shower, grateful once again for the invention of hot water. It only took about twenty minutes for them to be in the car and headed to the park. They were lucky enough to find a picnic area that wasn't too far from the frozen stream, making for a very picturesque lunch.

"Would you like to take a hike? It doesn't feel too cold out since the wind isn't strong today," Emma asked, cleaning up the remains from lunch.

"That sounds nice. Maybe we can walk to the waterfall. It may be completely frozen at this point," Doc suggested.

"I would love to see that," Emma exclaimed excitedly.

They stored the picnic basket and food in the SUV before walking up the trail. The dusting of snow was pretty but so far had not caused it to be too slippery. They walked slowly, enjoying the view, holding hands. Reaching the waterfall, it was indeed frozen, and Emma stopped to take some pictures of it, including a selfie of the two of them. She wanted Albert to have pictures of his first birthday celebrations. Zooming in on the picture to make sure it was in focus, she saw something in the background. Enlarging it even more, she gasped.

"Albert! Look!" Emma pointed at her screen.

Doc took the phone to look at it. There appeared to be an animal of some sort lying on the ground in the rocks by the waterfall's pool. Looking up, it was hard to see it through the rocks, their fur blending well. "We can check it out but be careful. Most animals would be avoiding us right now." He checked with his beast, but it didn't seem worried. Probably not a predator then.

Inching their way closer, Doc stopped Emma when his beast let out a sad neigh. "Emma, I don't think she made it. I'll make sure, but you can stay here if you want." His Emma was tenderhearted, and he knew she would be sad an animal had died.

Emma shook her head. "I'll come with you."

They walked up to the animal, noticing it was a female wolf. It looked like she had been shot. He would have to report it to the game warden; there should be no hunting in the National Park. There were no signs of life, her eyes frozen open. Doc grabbed Emma, pulling her away abruptly as the stomach suddenly moved.

"What—? Albert, what is going on? I thought she was gone?" Emma asked, worried. If the animal was still alive, they had to find a way to help her. She would die out here in the cold if another animal didn't get to her first. Peering her head around her mate's back, she gasped as she saw a tiny pup wiggle out from under its mother. "Oh, he's so tiny! Albert, we need to help it," Emma cried.

Doc hummed, letting her know he heard her. He walked slowly closer, trying not to scare the little pup. It was young, probably still days old at best. He wasn't sure if the poor pup would make it, certainly not by itself. Wolf pups were born blind and deaf until around two weeks old. A scavenger would pick off this little guy in no time.

Emma rushed over, gently cupping her hands around the tiny, almost frozen body. Doc watched as she cuddled the pup to her chest, sharing her warmth. He leaned down to examine the body. She had definitely been shot. He wasn't sure what she was doing here either; wolves hadn't been seen in this area for many years. Rigor mortis had set in, but he felt along her stomach. She must have been trying to give birth or the shock of being shot prompted birth. The pup's siblings didn't make it out. He dropped a pin in his map so he could tell the game wardens where to go. Walking over to Emma, he noticed how she was cradling the wolf, speaking softly to it.

"We'll take care of you, yes we will. I'll have to find out what to feed you."

He didn't want to upset her, but the chance for its survival was low after being out in the elements, especially since its mother died. They could try bottle feeding, but it was still a wild animal.

Wolf. Dog. Both. Mate likes. Keep.

Doc sighed. Now his beast was giving his opinion. Leaning forward, he took in the pup's scent. He did smell like both a wolf and a dog. Maybe his mother had conceived with a regular canine. He would have to ask Sam what his wolf thought of it.

"Let's get him to Sam. He may be able to help. I really wish the vet hadn't retired and moved to Florida, we could use his help right now," Doc said as he helped Emma walk back to the SUV.

"Call Sam," Doc instructed as he began the drive back into town.

"Hey, Doc," Sam answered. Emma snorted quietly.

"Sam, can you meet us at the house? I need your help on something. Give Rolf a heads up too. Can you research what an abandoned wolf pup eats? Newly born, not very old, would still be on liquids."

"Wolf pup? What did you guys get into on your picnic?" Sam asked incredulously.

"We'll be home in about fifteen minutes, you'll see then," Doc replied. "Bye."

"Send message to Gage. Dead wolf found in National Park. She-wolf shot. Will send GPS location when I get home.

Can you let game wardens know? Send," Doc instructed his phone. He wanted the game wardens to know about the wolf, but he also wanted Gage to know as the acting paranormal law around here, that there could be hunters in the park. The shifters wouldn't be safe if that was the case. It might take a lot to kill a paranormal, but most of them could still die from a well-placed bullet.

Pulling into the driveway he saw Sam, Shaye, Rolf, and Gage waiting for them. Emma slid out, holding the little bundle snuggly.

"Let's go inside, he needs to be warm."

"I already have the fireplace going. Tess is inside making formula replacement since we don't have any. I think she ordered some real stuff online as well, but this should work in the short term," Sam said.

Doc nodded a greeting to Gage. Taking out his phone, he sent him the GPS location of the poor wolf. Everyone gathered next to the fireplace, where Emma sat with the little pup.

"What happened, Mom?" Rolf asked, leaning over to look at the sleeping wolf.

"We went on our picnic and decided to walk to see if the waterfall had frozen. I took a selfie and was checking to make sure it was in focus when I saw something in the background. We walked over to see what it was and found the poor mom had been shot. She was clearly a wolf, and on park lands. This little guy wiggled out from underneath her somehow."

"I would say the gunshot was what ultimately killed her. I don't think she was trying to give birth near the waterfall, I think her injuries probably induced labor. He was the only one that made it out. I didn't hear or scent anyone else near us, so she may have wandered there after being shot; although I don't think that she would have made it far with her injuries. We were far enough in the park that I think she may have been shot there, or at the very least close by. All the woods around here have a no-hunting policy, simply due to hikers. I know it's the game warden's or park rangers' jurisdiction, but I wanted you to be aware of it too, Gage. If someone is hunting close by, the shifters in town may be in danger as well."

"I'll send out a notice to everyone in town over the emergency alert. Humans shouldn't be in the woods if someone is shooting either. I will call the human authorities when I get back to the office and let them know," Gage replied.

Tess came out of the kitchen carrying a small bottle. "This was the smallest one they had at the store. It's for a human baby, but I ordered some animal bottles and the formula. They should be here in a couple of days." She had made an emergency formula out of milk, egg yolks, salt, and oil. Multiple sites had used the same ingredients, so she hoped it worked.

As Emma tried to get the pup to eat, Doc beckoned to Gage and stepped away from the group. "I took a few pictures in case the body disappears before they get there. I didn't sense anyone nearby, but I really do think she was shot in the park."

"I have no idea what she would have been doing up here either. We haven't had any reports of wolves or even coyotes coming near the livestock, so I don't believe it would be anyone from around here. The town is normally pretty good about spreading the word about predator sightings, if only to make sure they aren't chasing off any local shifters," Gage added.

"The placement of the shot would mean she would not have been able to travel far, another reason I think it was in the park," Doc added.

Gage nodded. Based on the pictures Doc sent, he would concur. "I'll send these along with a report to the authorities. I'll also make a reminder "No Hunting" flyer to hang in the public buildings. I truly don't think it was anyone local, which is concerning. I'll go check out the site as well and see if I can pick anything up. Let me know if you need any help with your new addition. And happy early birthday, in case I don't get a chance to see you tomorrow."

"Thanks," Doc replied, shaking Gage's hand. It was extremely helpful that they had become friends of a sort with the Sheriff. He knew the Sheriff was hiding something, but Doc would put money on it being something to do with his animal side. After hiding his for so long, he wasn't about to push the issue with anyone else. Gage would tell them if or when he was ready. "I'm not sure if we'll be able to keep him though. He's a wild animal at heart."

Gage cocked his head, drawing in a deep breath. "Hmm. Mom was a wolf, but dad seems to have been a dog. German Shepherd...or maybe a German Shepherd wolf mix himself. Sam might be able to scent it better. Anyone else I would say he would need to go to a wildlife sanctuary, but I think he will do well here. Talk to Sam, but I think the pup will be a good guardian for the estate. I'll let you know what I learn," Gage said as he went to the front door.

Doc went back to the living room, watching Emma coax the pup into eating. He silently cheered as the pup finally latched onto the nipple and slowly began to eat.

"Sam, what do you think? I sense part wolf, part dog. I know he can't survive on his own yet, but is there enough dog in him to be able to stay with the Clan or is it better for him to be released at a sanctuary?"

Sam knelt next to Emma. "Can you lift him up a little bit so I can scent him? I'm going to go shift and I'll be right back; I'll scent him better in my wolf form."

The pup had fallen asleep by the time Sam came back less than a minute later. His furry head looked huge compared to the tiny body. Sam's wolf sniffed the pup, rubbing his head lightly against his. A few moments later, he left to shift and came back.

"Definitely some dog in there. German Shepherd would

be my guess. A lot of German Shepherds have some wolf in their DNA already, due to breeding generations back. He has enough dog in him that he could be trained and form attachments to us. The big difference between us and a regular human family is that we are a Pack, a Clan, a tribe. A lot of us are what would be the alpha in a Pack, so he would have leadership to follow. He would need a lot of training, which considering someone is always here, should be fine. We would also need to socialize him, since the wolf side of him will potentially be skittish around other dogs and people. As soon as his eyes open, we should start with socialization; bring him to the pet store, the dog park, walk him around town to get used to noises and people. It's actually a good thing Rolf installed the stupid dog-door for me, since this guy will probably like roaming the property. If Emma was the first scent he has besides his mother's, he may already be forming a bond to her, which should help us train him.

"It will be like having newborn baby; everyone should wash their hands before holding him and he will eat frequently. I know a vet friend who I will ask to visit when he is old enough for shots," Sam added.

Shaye ran to the kitchen to throw a roast in the oven for dinner and they all took turns holding and feeding the pup throughout the night; even Gawain took a turn when he heard there was a puppy downstairs. The pup did end up sleeping in their room though, Doc thought wryly. He didn't think Emma would let him out of her sight any time soon.

15

Doc walked downstairs, still a little bleary-eyed. He had not gotten a lot of sleep last night due to the puppy feedings. He still had work though, so he trudged down the stairs to make some coffee. Tea just wasn't going to cut it today. He stopped short at the bottom of the stairs, looking at the balloons decorating the living room. He heard voices in the kitchen and headed that way.

"Good morning! Happy birthday!" Shaye said as she came over to give him a kiss on the cheek. "Your breakfast is almost done."

Doc sat on a barstool, looking at his family. Berkley was flipping what smelled like sausages while Ian was at the coffee machine. "What am I eating?" Doc asked, amused.

Tess came up behind him, placing a crown on his head. "Fresh blueberry muffins, sausage and/or bacon, and scrambled eggs. Happy birthday," she added, kissing his cheek.

"Thank you, that sounds wonderful."

He enjoyed his breakfast with the other early risers and blew his sleepy mate a mental kiss before heading to work. Shaye and Tess decided to drive in together and were going to leave a few minutes after him. He always liked to have a few minutes to himself before the clinic opened to go over patient files. Doc was soon immersed in preparing for the day, making sure he didn't need anything special ordered like lab work. He could hear the girls talking as they came in and got ready for their first patient. A few minutes later, Sherri's voice joined in. It sounded like they were all over the office this morning. Sherri poked her head around his door.

"First patient in ten minutes, Doc," she informed him.

"Thanks. How was your weekend?" he asked.

"It was good, we just relaxed. Happy birthday," Sherri added as she rushed out the door with a laugh.

Doc sighed with a grin. The girls must have told her. He had always just said it was in the winter and she would randomly show up with a present on whatever cold day she felt like that year. It had been a fun game.

Heading into the first patient room, he caught sight of something colorful in the waiting room. He'd have to check it out later.

"Good morning, Stella. How are you today?" Doc asked one of his favorite patients. She had been coming to the clinic since she was a toddler. Although she was now ninety-five, she still had the mischievous twinkle in her eye and her sharp wits.

"Oh, I'm wonderful. I finally found out when your birthday is. All it took was ninety years and you finding your people," she huffed.

Doc laughed. She had asked him several times over the years, but he had always kept it vague. After all, how could he explain that he had no idea when his birthday was without people wanting to know the backstory. He had to admit though, it was nice being able to tell people a date if they asked from now on. He wasn't sure why he never thought of it before.

The rest of the day was similar, although Sam brought over lunch, including an extra side of veggies and sautéed apples just for him. When there were only a few patients left for the day, he took a break to check in with Sherri at the front desk. He hadn't had a chance to talk to her much today and he wanted to make sure she could read some of his notes for the electronic files.

"What in the world?" he asked as he walked into the waiting room. There were Happy Birthday balloons scattered throughout the area and he had a sneaking suspicion this was why everyone knew it was his birthday. He didn't see the girls, although he heard voices outside. Stepping out onto the porch, he saw Sherri, Tess, and Shaye talking to Mary who was holding a bakery box.

"Happy Birthday, Doc! I saw the sign up this morning and whipped up some cupcakes for your dessert tonight. You'll have to let me know how they are; it's a new recipe, lemon meringue cupcakes."

"Those sound delicious! I can't wait to try them," Doc said, peeking into the box. They did look good, lemon cupcakes with a vanilla buttercream and a pool of lemon custard peeking out from under a hat of torched meringue. "Oh, Mary. These look amazing. Thank you so much."

"I better get back; Bill is holding down the bakery on his own and he never hears the timer go off anymore. I already have a hearing test set up," she added with a smile when Doc opened his mouth. "Happy birthday, dear. Tell Emma I said hello," Mary added as she kissed Doc on the cheek and headed back to her bakery.

He looked at the front of his clinic, seeing the balloons and the "It's Doc's Birthday!" banner hanging off the front porch. "Well, I know why everyone told me Happy Birthday." He laughed. "Thank you," he told them. Walking back up the stairs, he saw a clipboard sitting on the railing. Reaching for it, he blinked when it disappeared before he could grab it.

"Nope, not for you yet," Tess laughed, hiding it behind her back.

Shaking his head, Doc headed back inside to finish the notes on the patient charts. When the last patient left, he hurried through the rest of his duties, wanting to get back home and sneak a cupcake. He had been good all day and resisted the temptation, but he could smell the lemon coming from the box, and he really wanted to try them. Shaye knocked and poked her head in.

"Everything's ready to close up. No eating a cupcake either," she teased. "You need to wait until after dinner. Ian said the brisket is ready as soon as we get home."

"Sounds good. Let me save these notes and I'll lock up."

"We'll wait. I've seen how you get distracted when you're working. You need to leave on time today, it's your birthday. Come on, Dad, let's go," Shaye said as she turned around.

Doc felt his heart skip a beat. It was the first time she had called him Dad, which he guessed he was, at least a father-in-law type. His beast smugly said *Mine.* Tossing his pen down on the desk, he shut down his computer and locked the cabinet full of his notes. He followed the girls home, where balloons decorated the front gate. At this rate, everyone in town would know it was his birthday. Walking into the house, he took a deep breath. It smelled delicious.

"How was your day?" Emma asked, carrying the pup, leaning up to give him a kiss.

"It was good. The girls decorated the office, so everyone knew it was my birthday. Mary sent home some cupcakes that look delicious. Two words…lemon meringue," Doc said conspiratorially.

"Oh, that does sound good! I'm getting very hungry; it's been torture smelling the brisket all day. Ian has been working on some leather goods in the back as he keeps an eye on it. I made some rolls and a few sides to go with it, plenty of vegetables and some baked apples too. Shaye gave me the recipe for those roasted Brussels sprouts that you love.

"The pup has been eating well today. We really need to

pick out a name for him. Did you have anything in mind?" Emma asked him.

"Hmm, nothing sticks out right now. Maybe when his personality starts to come out more, I'll have some ideas," Doc answered. It had been a long time since he had to come up with a name for something. He would be useless when it came to naming any children they had.

"Dinner's ready!" Ian shouted from the kitchen.

"Let's eat," Emma said, grabbing his hand and dragging him into the kitchen.

They had a delightful dinner, followed by a short game night, where Doc kicked everyone's butts in a game of *Ticket To Ride*. He even got a few new editions for his phone and some new board games. Rolf told him he was putting in some wide hiking trails so he could run easier in his horse form, as well as the non-shifters who might want to explore the woods. It was a nice relaxing night, perfect for his first birthday celebration. Shaye and Tess presented him with a large card that had notes and signatures from his family and many of the townspeople. This must have been what Tess had hidden on the clipboard, he thought to himself. He had to clear his throat before he could tell them thank you; it was extremely touching to know that he meant so much to the people in the town.

Doc ran into the kitchen, grabbing the cupcakes to share with everyone. He took a minute to breathe. He hadn't known what he had been missing out on before this family came to him.

"I was going to bring out some ice cream. I wasn't sure if you wanted to share your gift," Shaye said, coming into the room. She started making coffees and tea.

"There are enough cupcakes for everyone. Although ice cream does sound good as well," Doc replied.

"We can have both. Birthdays are meant to have lots of dessert, or so I'm told," Shaye replied with a smile.

"Well, in that case, maybe we can bring out the toppings for sundaes too," Doc suggested.

"Sounds perfect. If you want to bring out the cupcakes, I'll start scooping ice cream into bowls. I have some candles to put on the cupcakes for you too."

"I don't think there is enough room for the number of candles we would need, nor do I think that the house wouldn't go up in flames," Doc replied, laughing.

"Well, we can just put one on for you to blow out, it's a birthday tradition to make a wish."

"Oh, you definitely have to make a wish on your birthday," Berkley agreed as he came into the kitchen. "I'm here to help carry. What can I bring out?"

"Can you get the drinks? I have a little pitcher of creamer in the fridge, and I put the sugar by the cups."

"I can do that," Berkley replied, loading the drinks onto a tray, and bringing it out into the living room.

The cupcakes tasted as good as they looked. The perfect end to the dinner. It was getting a little late and everyone had work in the morning, so couples started meandering off to bed. As they walked up the stairs, Emma handed off the pup to Sam and Tess. "They're going to watch him tonight so we can have some…alone time," Emma replied to the unspoken question on Albert's face with a blush.

"Oh! I am very tired, let's go to bed," Doc said as he started walking faster up the stairs, loving the sound of Emma's laugh.

Emma went into the bathroom to change. She wanted to make Albert's birthday special and had bought an outfit for tonight. It wasn't as risqué as some of the ones she saw the girls shopping for, but she liked it. Putting it on, she looked in the mirror. She brushed out her hair, leaving it down. Her pale pink, almost-sheer negligée was held up by spaghetti straps and reached down to the tops of her feet. Other than being close to see-through, it was the deep leg slits on either side that really made it sexy. The slits went all the way to her hips, giving tantalizing glimpses of her lace panties underneath when she walked. She wore hot pink ones to stand out a bit from the gown. Emma had even painted her toenails a pale purple this morning while the pup was sleeping.

Opening the door, her breath caught at how handsome Albert was. He was lying on the bed, in just his underwear. He had on snug black boxer-briefs today. His white hair shown in the low light and his dark eyes filled with heat as he looked at her.

"You look amazing," Doc said, his voice a little deeper and raspy. Emma watched as his cock began to fill. "Come here," he beckoned holding out a hand.

Emma laughed as he tossed her underneath him, quieting quickly as he pressed a kiss to her lips. Grabbing his hair, she pulled him in for a deeper kiss, her tongue teasing his lips. His tongue rubbed slowly against hers, his hands caressing her body. She felt her nipples harden and he moved his mouth down to lightly suck on one through the fabric. The other breast was teased as he lightly fondled it. The slight abrasion of the fabric was delicious and soon she was panting, her nipples the hardest they had ever been.

"Albert. I need…" Emma loved what he was doing but it seemed like he was going slowly tonight, taking his time as he worked his way down her body. He gently pressed kisses down her chest and stomach, moving the middle piece of fabric out of the way to reach her vulva. Pausing above her mons, he breathed in deeply, drawing in the aroma of her desire. He loved being able to turn her on, she could feel his satisfaction and desire through their bond. She watched as his dark eyes met hers, full of love and passion, moving her underwear down, he held out his tongue, licking along her slit. Her lips plumped, blood rushing to them as her arousal increased. Albert licked gently along her clit, her hips chasing the sensation. He teased her though, only lightly caressing it, little butterfly kisses. She needed it harder, more pressure, more to fill her up, something. Finally, just as she was about to grab his head and shove him down there, he slid a finger into her waiting heat. "More, Albert. Stop teasing me," she demanded.

"I'm not teasing, I'm savoring. I'm loving," he replied, amusement in his voice.

"Love faster," she replied, desperate to feel him inside her. For something that had terrified her, she now craved it with Albert. He always made sure to make her feel safe, to feel desired, and she loved it.

He responded by gently thrusting three fingers into her channel, his tongue flicking against her clitoris. It was amazing, but the gentle caresses were only ramping up her lust, not even coming close to sating it. She pulled his head up by his hair. "My turn," she snarled. "Lie on your back."

As her cocktease of a mate lay down, she drew his penis out of his underwear, leaning down to lick the precum leaking from it. Climbing up his body, she straddled his waist. Grasping his shaft with one hand, she balanced on his chest with the other. She dragged his dick through her folds, teasing her clit with his heat, drenching his length with her wetness. Emma grinned down at Albert when she felt his muscles tense beneath her. She slowly slid his cock into her, her inner muscles grasping, drawing him in. As her butt finally touched the top of his legs, she sat there for a minute enjoying the sensation of being full. Leaning forward to kiss him, she gasped as the new angle stimulated her G-spot. Her tongue thrust into his mouth, kissing him deep as her hips started to grind against him. Albert's hands gripped her hips tightly. Her orgasm rushed through her as she felt his cock swell inside her and fill her with his heat.

Lying there, both of them breathing heavily, but utterly satisfied, Doc grunted as his phone beeped. He ignored it until it blared a warning sound, the one he had set up for alerts on the forum site. Kissing Emma's forehead, he rolled over to grab his phone. There was a notification from the forum about a new private post.

"What is it? Is there an emergency at the clinic?" Emma asked.

"No, it's from the forum. Anonymous1 sent me a private message."

Emma leaned into his back. "What does he want?"

Doc opened the message, almost dropping his phone in shock when he saw pictures of a document.

"Emma, look." His hand was shaking so badly that she took the phone from him. Her gasp matched how he was feeling.

Anonymous1: *Happy birthday. Hope this helps. Glad you found your own tribe/Clan.*

Doc read with Emma. It was what they had been looking for. The answer to help keep their kids safe forever.

"How did? Who?" Emma floundered.

Doc shook his head. He had no idea who Anonymous1 was or how they knew it was his adopted birthday. The only people who knew were in town. Unless… No, it was better to focus on this. He could finally talk to his family and see if they wanted to share in his immortality.

EPILOGUE

Emma was sound asleep, she knew she was. But this dream was so realistic, other than the haziness around her. Jacob stood in front of her, his kind eyes full of brotherly love.

"Jacob! I've missed you," Emma cried, rushing toward her friend. It was her dream, but she was still shocked when she was able to hug him. "I'm sorry I haven't talked as much lately. I got caught up in life here. But I never forgot you," she promised.

"Don't be silly. I know that. I've been watching over you. I am so glad you finally found someone to let in. It's everything I could have wanted for my dearest friend."

"What about you? Are you alright? You aren't earthbound, are you?" Emma questioned, worried.

"No, not earthbound. I just like to check in on you and make sure you're okay. I can hear you when you talk to me and sometimes I'll come close, but I'm not stuck here. I was hoping I would be able to find a way to contact you, and I finally had someone to help," Jacob said with a grin.

"Are you happy?" Emma asked softly, tucking her head down on his shoulder like they used to sit at the farm.

"I am. I have someone I wanted to introduce you to," Jacob said. "He helped me figure out how to reach you. He's nice, I swear," Jacob promised. He knew she had made great strides in being more comfortable around people, but he also knew Terrance was huge. The man was seven feet tall and muscular. He could be intimidating if you didn't know him.

"Oh! I'll have to tell him thank you."

Jacob looked over his shoulder and beckoned.

"Emmaline, I would like to introduce you to my other best friend. My mate."

Emma's head came up so fast she almost smacked it into Jacob's chin. "Your what?"

"My mate. He's a bear shifter. We met in the afterlife. How crazy is that?" Jacob bounced on his toes in excitement. He was finally able to introduce his dearest friend to his partner. The two people in the world who cared about him were finally meeting.

Emma looked at her friend closely. She had no idea such a thing was possible, but there was a mating mark on his neck. "I am so happy for you," she replied, tears in her eyes.

"It is very nice to meet you," she said, holding out her hand to greet Jacob's person. She didn't think she was ready for a hug just yet. "Jacob is amazing. Did he tell you that he saved my life? I am so happy he finally found someone to love him, because he deserves all the love," Emma added fiercely.

"Do you want to sit and talk?" Jacob asked as a couple of couches, a coffee table, and four teacups appeared.

"I would love to," Emma replied, sinking into the couch. "Is someone else coming?" she asked, looking at the fourth cup.

"I wanted to meet Albert if you thought he would be amenable. I can teach you how to bring him in," Jacob replied.

Emma nodded. Having Albert here would be good. She felt a little discombobulated at the moment.

"Focus on him through your mate bond and find his dreaming conscious. Gently tap to get his attention and if he wants to come, have him follow you here."

Moments later, Albert appeared in the dream.

"Albert! This is my friend Jacob and his mate Terrance. They met in the afterlife, can you believe it?"

"It's very nice to meet you both," Doc said, leaning forward to shake their hands. It certainly looked like Jacob based on Emma's description and the portrait she had of them.

'Love, I really hate to ask, but are you positive this is Jacob? I want to make sure it's not someone trying to attack you.' Doc asked, using their telepathic bond.

'It's him. He has the same mannerisms and the scar he got from the rooster on his hand,' Emma replied. It hadn't even crossed her mind that it could be anyone but Jacob.

"Terrance, did Jacob ever tell you about his nickname?" Emma asked.

"No, I don't think he did," he replied, glancing down at his mate in amusement.

"Emma, don't you dare," Jacob warned.

"One day, he was helping with the chores. He was trying to feed the chickens, but the rooster we had at the time was an asshole. He never liked people near his girls. He got out of his pen and started chasing Jacob around the yard. Jacob slipped in some...we'll just call it mud, but it was really close to the cow pens... Anyway, he slips and falls on his butt, the feed bucket goes flying in the air, landing on his head like a hat. The bucket had been full, so now all the hens are swarming him. He's sitting there in cow pies and surrounded by hens, so I called him Henny Pie."

"It's how I got this scar on my hand. The stupid rooster

took a chunk out. He wasn't even trying to get food, he just wanted to attack me for being close to the hens," Jacob added.

What seemed like hours passed as they talked and learned about each other. Emma knew it was almost time to wake up, but she was sad to leave her friend behind.

"Will we get to meet like this again?" Emma asked. "If I have Albert's immortality, I won't see you in the afterlife. I don't want to lose you a second time. I know you have your own life now too." She sniffed, holding back tears. It was amazing and awful at the same time that she got to see her friend.

"You have your own life to live, it will be so great to watch. Your life is going to be so full, long, and full of love and family and happiness. You don't need me anymore," Jacob replied gently. He hated that his friend was hurting, but he had seen glimpses into her future, and it was everything he could have wanted for his Emma. He didn't want to lose her either, but he could keep checking in on her.

"I will always need you, dork. You are my dearest friend." Emma gently smacked him on the arm.

"Well, then we will have to try this again," Jacob promised, grabbing his mate's hand. "I love you, Emmaline. I am so happy for you."

"I love you too. I always wanted you to be happy, and I am so glad you finally had that chance," she replied, giving Jacob a hug. "Thank you," she told Terrance, giving him a quick hug as well.

Stepping back, she grabbed Albert's hand, smiling as he gently squeezed it in support.

"It was nice meeting you both," Doc said. "I look forward to next time."

Jacob and Terrance waved before slowly disappearing.

Emma woke up with a gasp, shaking Albert awake.

"Albert! Wake up!"

His eyes opened and slowly focused on her. "That was

your Jacob?" Doc asked. "I am glad I was finally able to meet him. Are you alright?" It's not often your deceased best friend visits in a dream and introduces his own mate.

"I am. I am so relieved, so happy that he found his own happiness and his own person to love."

"Do you want to go back to sleep or get up?" Doc asked. He was wide awake, but if Emma wanted to go back to sleep, he would lie there and hold her.

"Hm, no I'm awake now, but I don't want to go downstairs yet. I have something I want to try first," Emma said, her eyes full of mischief. She started scooting down under the covers, slowly drawing Doc's sleep pants down.

"Oh! I'm fine spending the morning in bed," he agreed as he felt her tongue reach out to lick his length.

Sunday nights were the best; it was when everyone was able to get together and share dinner. Doc felt like he got to touch base with most of the family at their Sunday dinners. He occasionally saw Sam in town during lunch, Tess and Shaye worked with him. Ian and Berkley sometimes would stop in to say hi and to have a chat, but Rolf worked from home and Gawain was normally holed up in a corner working on his research. Doc had given him a few ideas to follow up on. He didn't want to call them leads because it had been so long since he had interacted with anyone from the old tribe or even looked for their old homesteads. Merri was a little better, as she recently started working part-time at the library, so Doc was able to see her in town. Merri was also the one who normally came downstairs to grab food for dinner. She brought Gawain's up to him but made him join them all for Sunday dinner.

Ian and Berkley waited until dessert to share their news.

"We finally set a date to see my parents. We'll be leaving in a couple of weeks," Ian said.

"I'm going to close the shop while we're gone and put a notice on the online shop," Berkley added. "I don't want you guys having to cover while I'm out. It's normally the slow part of the season, so it would just be a lot of sitting around."

"You'll have to send us pictures," Shaye said. "I want to go see Scotland, especially Loch Ness, one day. And make sure you let us know when you land!" With attacks on Rolf and Tess and Sam, she was both happy Ian would be able to see his family, but worried that they would be so far away. She could sense everyone in the Clan's well-being, at least within a couple hundred miles, but had no idea if her reach would extend across the ocean.

"I will send you so many pictures!" Ian promised. He couldn't wait until they could plan a big family trip and see his home country. Maybe they could fit in England on that trip too. He was sure Berkley and Emma had plenty of places to show them.

Doc looked at Emma, who nodded in return. "I know you guys are leaving soon, but before you go, there is something we wanted to talk to you about," Doc said, placing his fork down and grabbing Emma's hand.

NOTE FROM THE AUTHOR

Thank you for reading *Pointed Love*! If you enjoyed the story, please leave a review. Reviews are invaluable to independent authors, and I value each one.

Keep reading for a sneak peek into *Forged In Love*, book four of the Nightwood Clan series. This book will focus on Ian and Berkley.

You can find a character list in the back of the book as well.

Agapi mou (αγάπη μου) means "my love" in Greek.

SNEAK PEEK: IAN AND BERKLEY

(FORGED IN LOVE, NIGHTWOOD CLAN, BOOK 4)

Ian woke slowly, stretching his arms above his head. His wrist glittering in the morning sun. Rolling on his side, he watched his love sleep. Berkley was everything he could have asked for in a partner; he was kind, hot as hell, creative, and helped balance Ian's own exuberance. He loved seeing the matching band on his mate's wrist. It was a collaboration between the two of them; Ian had made the leather bracelets and Berkley had made the center stone. It was a gorgeous bead that was spelled not to break. Ian could feel a few other protective spells on it. He never took it off, the spell keeping the leather safe even in the shower.

His stomach was a bit of a mess though. He was excited to see his parents again. They didn't even have home internet, so it had been mostly letters and a few phone calls over the years. His aunt and uncle had given them such a great gift when they turned them, but his parents never really progressed past that time. Oh, they had a truck now, but only because they stood out too much if they brought a horse and wagon into town for supplies. They still tilled the land by animal and by hand, his da's forge sounded like a thing of beauty, but was definitely not modern.

His coming home would also sort of be his coming out. His parents knew in theory that he was gay, but he had never brought anyone home before. All trysts were kept far away from his parents. Once he came to America, he found it was easy enough to find a playmate when he needed one. He never let it get serious, knowing he could have a potential mate out there. His aunt and uncle were wonderfully supportive. Stepping in to act as his parents for his new identity, even trying to set him up on some blind dates. Talk about awkward, your "parents" trying to set you up, but he knew they were doing it to show their love and acceptance. When he met Shaye, his plans took a drastic turn. There was just something about the young human that made him stay and suffer through high school and college instead of leaving like he had originally planned. She had been his best friend, along with Tess and he was so incredibly happy to be with them again. Shaye had always been like a little sister to him, and now they were each other's family under the Clan.

Berkley grumbled in his sleep, reaching out to touch Ian. He always did this right before he woke up. Ian grinned to himself, lightly tracing his hand down his lover's back, admiring the muscles earned from working with clay all day. Of course, being Fae, he was also stronger and more on the lean side, but his man was certainly fine. Ian rested his hand on the swell of Berkley's ass before lightly smacking it. It had such a great bounce that he did it again to the other cheek.

"It's going to be one of those mornings, is it?" Berkley asked, his voice still rough with sleep, arching his ass up to meet Ian's hand.

"Mmhm," Ian agreed. "Did I tell you yet this morning that I love you?"

Berkley laughed. "I just woke up, so no."

"Let me make it up to you," Ian replied, his eyes twinkling. He disappeared under the sheet.

"Ung," Berkley groaned. "Turn around so I can say good

morning too," he begged, hoping Ian would sixty-nine this morning. He had never been a sexual person, but Ian certainly brought it out in him.

NIGHTWOOD CLAN

LOCATION

The series is mainly set in Rockfort, Tennessee, a fictional town.

CHARACTERS

Rolfston
Species: Vampire
Mate: Shaye
Job: Investments, day trading, Clan leader
Special Abilities: Telepathy, shielding
Book: Bite Me Again

Shaye
Species: Human/Vampire
Mate: Rolf
Job: Nurse
Special Abilities: Healing
Book: Bite Me Again

Sam
Species: Werewolf
Mate: Tess
Job: Owner, Black Wolf Brewery
Rolf's friend
Book: A Hairy Situation

Tess
Species: Witch
Mate: Sam
Job: Medical coding, nurse
Shaye's friend
Book: A Hairy Situation

Emma (Emmaline)
Species: Vampire
Mate: Doc (Albert)
Job: Landowner/small farm
Special Abilities: Visions/Premonitions
Rolfston's mother
Book: Pointed Love

Doc (Albert)
Species: Alicorn
Mate: Emma
Job: Doctor
*Special Abilities: Some healing, visions, magic,
    immortality*
Book: Pointed Love

Ian

Species: Vampire
Mate: Berkley
Job: Leathersmith, blacksmith
Special Abilities: Speed
Shaye's friend
Book: Forged In Love

Berkley

Species: Fae
Mate: Ian
Job: Owner/Potter, The Winged Potter
*Special Abilities: Can sense auras and species, slight
    healing ability*
Rolf's friend
Book: Forged In Love

Gawain

Species: Falcon shifter
Mate: Merri
Job: Historian/archeologist
Rolf's friend

Merri (Meredith)

Species: Witch
Mate: Gawain
Job: Librarian
Tess's sister

Vladimir

Species: Vampire
Evil father of Rolfston
Note: Appeared in Bite Me Again

Sheriff (Gage)
Species: Unknown
Mate: None (yet)
Job: Sherriff of Rockfort, Warden
Special Abilities: Very strong magic

Duncan
Species: Dragon
Note: Vlad killed his sister. Assisted in battle in Bite Me Again.

Sherri
Species: Human
Job: Receptionist at Doc's clinic

Marge
Species: Cat shifter
Job: Librarian in Rockfort

Marco
Species: Unknown
Job: Hunter for Wardens
Note: Collected the bodies of the men who attacked Tess and Sam. Appeared in A Hairy Situation.

Beth
Species: Human
Mate: Josh (witch)
Job: Florist/Owner, Rockfort Blooms

Samantha
Species: Brownie
Job: Caretaker for Emma's farm in England, weaves and quilts blankets
Note: Mentioned in Pointed Love

Douglas
Species: Gnome
Job: Ferrier, Sculptor, helps on Emma's farm
Note: Mentioned in Pointed Love

Thalia
Species: Unicorn
Job: Healer
Note: Deceased. Mentioned in Pointed Love.

Jacob
Species: Human
Mate: Terrance (bear)
Job: Farmhand
Note: Emma's friend, deceased. Mentioned in
  Pointed Love.

Terrance (Ter)
Species: Bear shifter
Mate: Jacob
Note: Deceased. Mate to Emma's friend Jacob (mated
  in afterlife).

ABOUT THE AUTHOR

I have loved reading since I was a child. I also enjoy baking, photography, and seeing new things. My favorite books are romances with a happily ever after. The world is a crazy place. Sometimes escaping into a great book is the only way I can truly relax. Happily ever after is my favorite type of book, so my stories will end with an HEA, even if the road is a little bumpy getting there. I travel a lot, but currently reside in the Midwest with my family.

Stay up to date with news, book release dates, special promotions and adventures, by visiting my website and social media pages.

www.HarperDakota.com
Harper's Readers Group

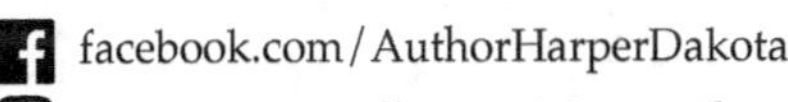

facebook.com/AuthorHarperDakota
instagram.com/harperdakotaauthor

ALSO BY HARPER DAKOTA

Nightwood Clan Series

Bite Me Again

A Hairy Situation

Pointed Love

Forged in Love